Listening And Speaking

NEW AND SELECTED STORIES

Ellen Wilbur

"These brilliantly crafted stories indulge in salient detail and proceed at a pace that gently leads to reversals at once contingent and fateful. Each piece invites and rewards multiple re-readings, which reveal how closeness rarely resolves into comfortable nearness, how proximity can often be most distant."

John T. Hamilton

"These are stories at once tender and unsparing; they have to do with those human beings whom life has damaged in mind, in psyche. Here the lost are given their understanding—these stories have found them. Skilled, sensitive, daring in their reach, they are clearly the work of a born writer."

Eudora Welty

"Some of Ellen Wilbur's stories take wing, as songs and lyric poems are meant to do; others remain earthbound for excellent reasons of their own. What they have in common is that all of them are told in a fresh, pure, original voice that deserves to be widely and gratefully heard."

Richard Yates

"Ellen Wilbur is an outstanding voice in fiction. She speaks in many tongues."

Gail Godwin

"It is as if a light shines through the stories of Ellen Wilbur. They are so marvelously clear, precise and yet profound in feeling; richly resonant and alive with an amazing marriage of subtle music and high energy. And yet the greatest wonder of all is their variety. She is a rare writer, in this age of so much uniformity and conformity, who can create many kinds and shapes of short fiction with ease and with equal art. She has great gifts and with this collection takes her place among the best of us."

George Garrett

"Ellen Wilbur's stories moved me as lovely music does: filled me with sorrow and loneliness, yet elevated me as well to the solitude where we receive the strength and blessing of art. Her music is her prose, and the heart it comes from."

Andre Dubus

"Ellen Wilbur's stories have a gravity, a graceful seriousness that makes them as satisfying as little novels. What intrigues me about her writing is that, without tricks or flamboyance, she goes in such unpredictable directions. One after another the stories turn out to be about something you didn't suspect when you began, something more fragmentary but usually more profound. My favorites… are complete and full of surprises of phrase and feeling.

Rosellen Brown

With deepest gratitude to George Garrett, Dewitt Henry, Patricia Traxler, and J.D. McClatchy for their unstinting help and encouragement over these many years.

First printing, April 2025
Library of Congress Control Number: pending
ISBN 978-1-953136-94-7 Hardback
ISBN 978-1-953136-00-8 Paperback

Cover Art, Design & Typography by **Kurt Lovelace**
Author's Photograph taken by **Michael Springer**
Cover *Bauhaus Dessau* Alfarn by Céline Hurka, Elia Preuss,
Flavia Zimbardi, Hidetaka Yamasaki, and Luca Pellegrini.
Body in **Nimbus**, Chapter Titles in **Jenson** by Robert Slimbach
Flourishes set in Emigre Foundry **Dalliance**, by Frank Heine
Emigre Foundry **ZeitGuys**, by Bob Aufuldish, Eric Donelan
Typefaces licensed Adobe, Linotype, & URW GmbH

PSPress.Pub
Pierian Springs Press, Inc
30 N Gould St, Ste 25398
Sheridan, Wyoming 82801-6317

for all in my family

CONTENTS

Listening And Speaking

RESCUE

The man and woman sit side by side in the front seat of the moving car. The man is driving. It is a warm, summer evening, and after a day of brilliant sun, the light has started to fade. This is their fourth date together. They've just finished a long dinner at a restaurant called The Captain's Club where they talked so much that until now they hardly have been silent for a moment. Both of them are thirty-nine years old and both are people who ordinarily speak very little. The man is known to be an eager listener, good at drawing other people out no matter how shy or quiet they might usually be. The woman falls silent early in most conversations, like someone crippled by a sudden shooting pain. All talk, no matter what the subject, soon reminds her of herself and something that she's missed or lacked in life, or wishes she could gain.

But this is not an ordinary night. Both the woman and the man can feel it. The choral music on the radio pours out with a poignancy and power that is surprising, and the air blowing through the open windows over their bare arms and across their faces has an exciting freshness. The woman's heart is beating hard. She puts her hand up to her chest to feel it pulsing, yet she isn't anxious, as she often is, about her body or her health. In fact she can't remember when she's felt so vital, like somebody sixteen, who has lost faith in nothing. They are driving up the shoreline. There is a sea view the man wants to show her, a view more beautiful than any he has seen.

The man is concentrating on the road, waiting for the crucial turn they must take. There is no space in his mind for thoughts of the life he's left behind in town, where he lives in a furnished studio apartment. His shirts hang drying out on hangers all around a room that is colorless and decorated only by the three framed photos on his bureau. There is a formal picture of his sister's three small children, one of his father as a young serviceman, and a color enlargement of a family gathering at his mother's house ten years ago. A musty smell hangs in the man's apartment, as though nobody lived there. He is a postal clerk during the day and moonlights as a car mechanic four nights a week. Often he eats his meals at fast food joints where he fills his stomach and hardly tastes the food.

People call on him for favors. Sometimes it seems that everyone who phones him wants his help. Weekends are always busy. He drives his aging aunts to church, to airports, to doctor's appointments, and takes his young nieces and nephews on outings to the zoo, museums, or the movies. He helps acquaintances to move and pitches in to paint their houses. People call him generous, yet he senses that they pity him. Beyond his car and clothing, he owns nothing. He has never married. He supports his mother as he's done for fifteen years, and now his aunt Noreen lives with her. He spends a good deal on his friends, buying their drinks, their baseball tickets, and dinners out. He rarely saves.

The woman could not be more different. She pinches pennies and is not overly concerned with other people's needs or wishes. Her own deep aches and longings constantly consume her. There is a darkness in herself that she's always escaping. It speeds behind her, like a vehicle that will hit her and destroy her if she ever slows enough to let it touch her.

She owns a flower shop, and for the past nine years she's poured all of her energy into the business, which has become tremendously successful. People say that no one in the area can touch her for the quality of her fresh flowers or the ingenuity of her arrangements. She's had to hire two new people just this month to handle the increasing volume of her clients. Yet she is happiest when she imagines how changed her life could be. She would like to dress more stylishly, to be more social, and to travel. She has never been abroad, and can't remember when she took her last vacation. She'd like to learn to ski in winter and play tennis in the summer: to have more fun. She wants to own a dog, to take horseback-riding lessons, and to live in a suburban house surrounded by wide lawns and flower gardens instead of the small condominium she owns in town. In fact, she has so many longings and unsatisfied desires that her private life seems almost worthless to her when she thinks of it, like a wasteland she feels paralyzed to change. She's had relationships with men, but she has never married, and soon she'll be too old to have a child. No matter how well she's done with her business, she only has to look at others to feel cheated and deprived.

And yet tonight, in the company of the man beside

her, she feels no envy. He is not like anyone she's met before. Everything about him is so large: his height, his broad, muscular shoulders, his lengthy arms, his huge neck, his deep, resounding laugh, and his great mouth, not only when it stretches into a wide smile, but its immensity when he is serious as well. All evening she has watched his mouth with fascination.

"Here it is," says the man as they turn from the highway onto a dirt road which curves up through a stretch of pine woods where the needles on the trees gleam in the softening light. The car emerges in a clearing and they head up a steep hill. The sky, banded with pink, is all they can see until they reach the top. They come to a stop, and the woman gasps at the extent of the view. On all sides before them the sea goes out to the horizon. The man turns off the engine, and the smell of salt blows through the car, where they sit staring at the airy splendor of the sky and water. The sun has fallen, but the scene is fully visible. The heavens are so cloudless, there will be a million stars to see from this high cliff tonight. The woman is quite speechless, feeling the impact of the view the way she felt the man's enormity across the table from her during dinner.

The man once had a long affair that ended hurtfully and badly. For many years he's been quite sure that he would never love again. Yet from the moment he entered the woman's flower shop a bare three weeks ago and met her, he's found himself drawn to her with increasing power. All week he has looked forward to this evening, and sensed her presence in his thoughts like a bright glow. Now she is beside him. Her face is tipped up to the light, her dark hair blowing out around her shoulders. Her hands are folded in her lap. It is her eyes that stir him: large, waif-like eyes that stare out with intensity. He supposes she isn't conventionally pretty, but she has a charm that seems to grow minute by minute, the way the dark is slowly gathering and building in the air around them.

"Lynn," he says. When she turns to look at him, he kisses her for the first time. In the dusky light they fall together and cannot stop kissing. The man is not prepared for the fiery feelings that overcome him. Soon he is breathing hard, and can feel how his excitement stirs the woman, who twists and turns her body in his arms.

In the past the woman has always been hesitant in her first embraces with a man, as though she needed to control exactly what she meted out to anyone who touched her. Tonight she keeps offering her mouth, pressing her body up to the man's. Gently, she bites his lip, blows softly in his ear, like someone calling to the deepest hidden part of him. She can feel him trembling as he holds her. She lets her head fall back. Her hair fans out behind her on the seat. He's leaning over her, the sounds of sea gulls and the salty air a part of every kiss, and it's at that moment when they hear a high-pitched voice that seems to call from a great distance.

"Help!" the cry is repeated. In an instant the man has jumped up, out of the car, and the woman scrambles after him. They hurry to the cliff's edge and look down through the failing light at the curving beach below. No people are in sight. A small, black dog runs frantically back and forth across the sand.

"Look!" Lynn yells against the wind. She points to the water. Twenty yards from shore they see two flailing arms and a small head rising from the sea. The man's face twists into a frown. He is not a strong or a proficient swimmer, but he starts to run towards the dirt path that leads down to the beach.

"Ed!" Lynn calls. The word rips from her throat with a surprising force. "Be careful!" She follows him as though a string were tied between them and she'd been yanked forward the moment that he moved. Before she knows it, she is pounding down the curving path behind him, her mind like a crowd of sirens going off together, warning her to watch herself, her fear of heights, the steepness of the stony, rutted hill, her proneness to sprains and injuries of every kind, her spells of dizziness, her asthma. She is *running too fast*, a siren is saying, and from the corners of her eyes she sees the world heaving with motion: the inward/outward movements of the sea, the zigzag of the barking dog, and the man shrinking beneath her as he trips, slides, leaps and hurtles down the hill with a ferocity of purpose that is horrible and thrilling to behold.

All during his descent Ed has focused on the person in the water, who has disappeared beneath the surface and then risen back to view. It's not until he's jumped onto the beach and the small black dog is racing towards him that he sees the swimmer is a child. A boy's head, plastered with water, rises from a wave before it sinks from sight. Ed propels himself across the sand with a new urgency. Passing the dog, he lunges towards the ocean with tremendous strides.

Lynn's new, black flats have been a hindrance, making her skid and slide the whole way down the hill. She kicks them off the moment she lands on the beach and runs barefooted over the sand, feeling the wind whip at her face and send her hair up flying while she watches Ed, who has now entered the water and become small against the backdrop of the sea. The black dog sees her and starts bounding towards her, barking. There is trash strewn here and there across the beach, beer cans and paper wrappers that make her want to watch for broken glass. In the fading light the ocean looks ink black and choppy. She can see no sign of the swimmer, yet Ed moves forward out to deeper water with strokes that are awkward and thrashing, and troubling to her to watch.

Ten miles away in town, as though she senses that

her son has put himself at risk, Ed's mother is thinking fixedly of him. She is sitting in her living room. Noreen, her elder sister, is beside her on the couch. They are both knitting sweaters for the church bazaar. The television news is on. The mother's face is calm, but inside she is anxious. She's thinking how unfulfilled and limited her son's life has become, her darling boy, whose goodness never seems to be sufficiently rewarded. When she thinks of the burden she has been to him, she freezes inside. She holds her breath tight in her chest and wishes she could die. Often she torments herself this way. Were she alone tonight, she'd throw herself down on her bed and cry. But it would be thoughtless to upset Noreen, who seems to have no horror whatsoever that her nephew is supporting them. Without Ed they'd probably be living on the street, but here they sit, two white-haired sisters, seventy-nine and eighty-two years old, long after they've fulfilled all earthly purpose, still eating, sleeping, using up the world's space and supplies, so that each breath they take is tantamount to greed. This is the way Ed's mother thinks tonight while her sister knits and hums a tune beside her. Noreen, Ed's favorite aunt, has put some brownies in the oven and the smell of them is drifting out and filling up the room with such a strong, rich fragrance that soon Ed's mother puts her knitting down. She stands and walks out to the kitchen to make their evening tea.

❧ ❧ ❧

From the moment he began to swim Ed's only thought has been that he must hurry if he is to save the child. Oblivious to the ragged gasps of his own breathing, he's pushed himself like an accelerator pressed down to the floor. There's a pain in his side and a tight stiffening in his left calf, yet he keeps swimming out.

Unless he has misjudged the distance, he is sure he must be near the boy, but there's no sign of the child. The light is almost gone now, and it's impossible for him to see far. He pauses, treading water, aware of the heavy weight of his wet clothing as he cranes his head to look around him. The ache in his side is sharper now, his leg is cramping badly, and he can't get his breath. Each inhalation is a struggle. His ears are filled with the commotion of his breathing, and when he turns to look, he cannot see the shore. The only light left in the air seems to have gathered close around him. It's falling down on him in a pale shaft, illuminating his white arms and shoulders, shining out from him as though he's never been the focus of such terrible importance. He coughs and sinks until he's choking, struggling to stay above the surface with the useless weakness of his body. This is where his life is going to end, he thinks. And what will happen to his mother?

Lynn is standing at the water's edge with the small dog leaping at her legs. One minute Ed is there and the next he's disappeared. There is nobody to be seen across the water. "Ed!" she cries. She calls his name repeatedly, moving down the beach with the dog behind her, feeling the panic rising in her body. "Where *are* you?" she keeps shouting, but there is no answer. The sound of her own voice trails off, and in an instant the whole ocean has become a wall of blackness.

❧ ❧ ❧

In the days after Ed's death, people keep calling Lynn, barraging her with questions. Ed is the town's hero. Their last evening together has exploded out in news across the country. She's met the parents of the child he tried to save, a boy of nine named Tommy Greer, whose body was recovered just a few yards from Ed's body. She's learned the name of the dog, Jasper, who followed her as she ran from the beach and found her way, falling and crying, up to the cliff top through the darkness, and out to the road, where she stood waving and screaming until she managed to flag down a car.

Ed's mother and his Aunt Noreen came right away to see her, both of them in shock and crying, reaching out to touch her, as though she were some remnant of Ed. "Did you know him long?" his mother asked, wanting to know the details of what happened, but asking her obliquely, unlike the police, who pounded her with questions for half an hour.

The whole town turned out for Ed's wake and funeral. He had so many relatives and friends with years of stories and events they could relate. Lynn couldn't help but think how little she had known him. So many people looked bereft, it stunned her. While people wept in all the rows of the packed church, she felt Ed had become a stranger to her. The tears she shed were for her own shock and confusion more than his death. It was the same at the boy's funeral, which she also went to: the anguished faces, the heart-sickness, prayers, testimonials and tears with television cameras poised outside the cemetery gates.

After the burial, she went home by herself, refusing the people who offered to stay with her. When she arrived at her place, she stripped off her clothes and stepped into the shower, letting the water pour over her head and body, scrubbing her hair and soaping every inch of skin, as though she could wash out the darkness and disaster that were in her. With hot water beating on her neck and shoulders, she thought of Jerry Butler, one of the policemen who had questioned her. He'd gone to high school with her in Bar Harbor, when she'd been a fearless swimmer. All through her teens she'd won trophies for the school and ribbons at the beachside competitions every summer. Jerry was surprised she hadn't tried to save the boy with Ed, and that it hadn't once occurred to her to enter the water. When she explained to him that she hadn't been swimming or visited a beach for years, he still looked unconvinced and shocked. In high school they had never known each other well, yet he seemed to remember her quite clearly. When the questioning was finally over and she stood up to leave, he waved her off and didn't look at her. His eyes were downcast, staring at his desk, and he didn't say a word.

THE NEW YEAR

At the Enright Company, where I worked, I was perceived by everyone to be hardworking and reliable. Often I remained at the office until after midnight and was back by 9 a.m. the following day. It didn't bother me that my whole life was focused on this job. I'd always been a person of extremes, and I found it oddly soothing to be driven through each moment by a single-minded purpose. For the past week I'd given up most socializing, and felt lucky to have no outside interests to distract me.

I'd been at Enright for two years, and the more I learned about the business, the more excited and immersed in it I was. Some days my mind exploded with ideas, and I sat and stared, unseeing, at the view outside my office window. Time disappeared and in those moments, deep in thought, I felt light-headed and enthralled.

Christmas came and went like a hidden jet flying above the city clouds, and all I knew was the distant sound of its approach until, for an instant, the full roar of the holiday was loud and hovering in my ears before the noise dissipated, leaving behind a gulf of welcome silence. Now it was New Year's Eve. I had no plan to celebrate. All afternoon the weather had been freakish. There were periods of snow, high wind, and every now and then a burst of sleet or pounding rain until it seemed that all the elements were pummeling the city. I'd been at my desk for hours, working on a speech I was to give at a convention in St. Louis the following Wednesday. My thoughts flowed easily onto the screen before me and I marveled at myself, as I'd done many times in the past six months, as though I had become someone articulate and new; a person I didn't know. As I glanced out the window at the blinding weather, it seemed my head had never been so clear. People scurried miserably on the slippery street below while I sat sealed in silence at my desk, immaculate and dry, wearing a new, expensive suit. I'd left instructions not to be disturbed, and was startled by the buzzer on my phone. As I lifted the receiver, I was surprised to see how late it had become. The sky beyond the window was completely dark.

"Sorry to bother you, Sam," my assistant, Mary Aldridge, spoke quickly. "Your uncle is on line two. He says it's an emergency."

My uncle had never phoned me that I could remember, and at the sound of his deep voice, I rose to my feet. "Uncle Bill?" I said, amazed.

"Your mother is dying," he spoke flatly.

"Dying?" I half-whispered.

"She may not make it through the day," he said. His voice was cold. "May I tell her that you're coming?"

The phone in my hand began to shake so hard, I was afraid that I might break a tooth. "Of course I'll come," I said. "I'll come right away."

"She's at St. Elizabeth's," my uncle said. "In critical care." There was a click as he hung up.

I stood by my desk, looking at a heavy swirl of snow illuminated by the streetlights far below, and for a moment I was unable to move. My past had been so buried, so dead asleep within me, it seemed as though I had been living on entirely without it. Now the present world melted away. There was no floor beneath my feet, and I couldn't feel the desk I leaned against. After a hurried call to my boss, I prepared to leave. The weather was so threatening, no planes were flying out of town. I put on my coat, grabbed my briefcase, shut the office door behind me, and hurried past my colleagues with eyes averted, unable to speak or tell them what had happened. The receptionist glanced up as I went by, but we said nothing.

Outside the building I managed to flag down a cab. "This is an emergency," I said to the driver, and I urged him to get me to the train station as quickly as he could. Before I knew it, I'd passed through a long line, bought a ticket for the two-hour ride, and was on the train.

I dropped my coat and briefcase on the seat beside me, hoping to discourage anyone from sitting there, and for the first hour of the trip I sat so still, it seemed that I was hardly breathing, staring wide-eyed out the window. I wondered how my uncle had located me. I hadn't called my mother or communicated with her since I'd disappeared from home eight years before, inspired by my brother, Jack, who'd run away six months before me, cutting all family ties. I'd no idea where Jack was or what had happened to him.

When I thought of my mother now, I could not blame or criticize her to myself the way I used to. She was not irritable, angry with my brother Jack or me. She wasn't moody, joyous one week and miserable the next, shut up in her room in bed all day. She wasn't a loose woman with no idea who had fathered her two children or a drinker, who could not keep a job. I didn't think of how she came and went and came and went, inspiring love and heartbreak everywhere. No friend, no lover and no child could ever hope to permanently hold or keep her. She rushed forward blazing with affection, and then withdrew completely, like an ocean tide that left behind a giant stretch of beach. These were things I didn't think of. All negative thoughts of my upbringing were entirely erased, as though my mother's life depended on it. Instead, the love I had for her revealed itself to me.

I remembered her face, how beautiful it was. People on the street would turn to stare at her as though they didn't want to lose her image. Now, when I thought back on it, our kitchen looked warm and inviting. It was clean, and the refrigerator was well stocked. I saw my mother in a pretty apron, cooking supper, the table neatly set, and how she leaned forward with a beaming smile when Jack and I came home from school to hug us tight and kiss us. I saw us watching television, the three of us curled up together on the couch when I was small.

While I sat, unmoving in my train seat, it seemed that every good she'd ever done enveloped me. I remembered how funny she could be, how uncontrollably she made me laugh at times, and as my love for her appeared to grow each minute, my view of myself became more ugly and demeaning. Tension and anxiety spread throughout my body until my agitation was so great that I could not sit still. I rose and had to walk repeatedly up and down the aisle in front of all the passengers. Ordinarily, I was a person who liked to make a good impression and cared what people thought of me. That day it didn't matter to me in the least how I appeared. A conductor, his eyes stern and alarmed, approached me and asked me to sit down.

"My mother is dying," I said harshly. Then, leaving my

coat on the seat, I picked up my briefcase, and pushed past him out of the car. I began to walk the whole length of the train, doors opening and clicking shut behind me. Speaking to my mother in my mind, I said, "I'll give up everything if only you'll be alive to see me." Then, as though to prove my point, I detached the gold watch from my wrist, flung it down onto the floor, and kept going. I yanked off my hundred-dollar tie and hurled it into the air over my shoulder. A button popped off my new shirt when I tore at the collar. I held my briefcase tightly as I paused in the open air between two cars. Sleet beat against my face, the windy cold was bitter, and I could feel the slippery surface of the icy floor beneath me. I began to shake horribly, yet I could not go back to the warmth and comfort of the train. I wanted to suffer.

I began swinging my arms back and forth, tossing my head and moaning, and when I thought of my mother's face, I heaved the briefcase overboard with all my strength, my mind in a frenzy I had never known before. If I could prove that nothing mattered to me more than she did, maybe she would survive.

"Live, Mother!" I cried as I threw my comb, my pen, and the loose change in my pocket into the whirling darkness. But it wasn't enough. Nothing was enough. The whole sickness of my life opened up to me in the dark like a picture that kept getting larger and larger and clearer and clearer until I couldn't bear it. Then, as I stood in the punishing cold, I tore open my sports jacket, tossed it overboard, and was reaching for the wallet in my pant's pocket, when through the window of the car behind me I could see the conductor coming at a hurried pace. The thought of being spoken to or touched by him was more than I could stand. When he reached the door, I flung myself against it. At first I held it shut, but the man was tall and heavy, and when the door burst open, I flew backward, skidding across the icy floor, while the conductor dove at me and pinned my shoulders hard against the wall. I struggled violently, but he rammed his knee into my abdomen and held me tight and still. My breath was knocked away, and for a moment there was just the sound of his explosive gasps and my choking for air. His enormous, ugly face was inches from my own, fierce and glaring. I'd never seen a face I hated more with its giant nose and his ugly, yellow teeth. I could not stand to look at him, and shut my eyes. We said nothing. Minutes passed and he held me motionless, as though time had no meaning and the cold had no importance. At last my legs became so weak, I felt as if they would collapse, and when I tipped my head back to look up at him, the conductor spoke as though he saw the difference in me. "Are you ready to go in now?" he said. When I nodded, he pulled me forward, opened the door, and we entered the train. We walked together back through all the cars. I went before him like a prisoner, his hand planted firmly on my shoulder as he followed close behind. I offered no resistance and had no fight left.

When we reached my seat, he stopped me, leaned over to pick up my coat, and gestured to me to sit down. Handing me the folded coat, he settled in the aisle seat beside me. "We'll be arriving in the city soon," he said. I noticed that he had a brogue. "I'll be sitting beside you till we're there." He pulled out his cell phone and spoke to someone briefly. There seemed to be a roaring in my ears and I could not make out any word he said. I guessed he must be calling the police, and that I would be handed over to them the moment the train stopped. God only knew what would happen after that.

Without a word, I let my head fall back. The air in the car seemed stifling, yet instead of feeling warmed, I began to shiver. I felt quite sure I'd never see my mother. By the time I reached the hospital, she would be dead. I was sure she'd died while I was on this train. I could feel it. The urgency was gone. It was as though I'd run twenty miles on an empty stomach or laid down for a short nap and slept too long, so many hours that waking now the mood of the whole day had changed.

I allowed myself to ponder things that were forbidden an hour ago. I wondered if my mother had been outraged and furious with me all these years, the way she'd been about my brother's disappearance, which struck her as an unforgivable betrayal. Jack was eighteen when he left, a thin, tall boy, almost six feet. He'd failed at school and taken up with a bad crowd. His last year at home, he'd distanced himself. Some days we hardly spoke, like people who had nothing but shame in common. He spent more time out with his friends than he did at home, and when he left for good, my mother would not speak of him. It was as though he'd never been. She began to tell me that she had a special love for me. She'd always favored me, she said, once Jack was gone.

I wondered if she had been crushed with pain and lonely all these years. There was no way to know. Always I had blamed myself for abandoning her, and yet she'd never tried to reach me.

"I can't live here anymore," I wrote in the note I scribbled at the kitchen table that January morning when I said my last farewell. My mother's sister, Anne, who was a history teacher, and her husband, Karl, an engineer, had urged me to move in with them for years. They knew how bad the situation was at home, and they had no children of their own. In my note I told my mother where I'd be, knowing she'd never forgive her sister or speak to her again. I remember standing in the frigid kitchen, looking at the words I'd written. My mother had been gone for two days with a new lover. She'd disappeared like this before, and I expected she would soon return. It was clear that once again she hadn't paid the bills. There was no heat. The room was freezing. The telephone had been shut off and the refrigerator was almost empty. That day I took a suitcase with me on the bus and a heavy satchel stuffed with my belongings. Anne was going to pick me up from school that afternoon.

Glancing at the conductor, I was surprised to find him dozing. The sight of his face no longer was repulsive, and I realized that I had become emotionally numb. Nothing could bother or upset me anymore. If a man stood in the aisle right now and shouted curses at a woman, I imagined it wouldn't move me in the least. Whether my mother was alive or dead, what difference would there be? This was how cold and utterly untouchable my heart seemed. And yet the moment the train began to slow and I could see that we were entering the city, I was overcome with anguish. Bells were ringing as we came into the station. The conductor awoke, reached into his jacket pocket, pulled out my watch, the tie I'd thrown away over my shoulder, and handed them to me as he rose to his feet. He looked down at my ravaged face.

"It's a terrible thing to lose your mother," he said, tapping my shoulder. Then he walked out of the car.

I stood in my coat on the chilly platform, felt for the wallet in my pocket, and was grateful that I hadn't thrown it overboard. There were empty taxis waiting in a line outside the station, yet I decided to walk the eight blocks to the hospital. The air was cold and dark, but the weather here was clear without a sign of ice or snow upon the ground.

I knew the city well, and exactly how to reach my destination. My mind kept pace with every step I took. I'd never thought of death so frightfully or squarely as I did now, and I could feel the struggle in my brain, as though it wanted to pave out a path towards every possibility that lay ahead. Tomorrow was the New Year, yet I moved forward slowly on the sidewalk, inching towards the past.

THE FORTUNE TELLER

Every breath you take is critical and every heartbeat in your chest is crucial. The state of all your organs is important, like a chorus where no voice can stand apart or overwhelm the rest or fail. A healthy person doesn't have to concentrate entirely on the body, while someone ill or badly injured never can ignore it.

Just listen to me, please, no matter how I seem to skip through time and subject matter. I'll talk about your past, specific memories you thought were yours alone. You'll learn how well I know you, all of your life up to the present moment and everything that lies ahead.

Do not be frightened by my words. Once we're finished, you will be a different person than before, not quite the same at all, the way each moment changes everything that is. When you leave today, you won't remember much that I have said, and yet you'll be suffused with a new strength, which will remain alive in you and never be destroyed.

You are the youngest of five children in your family. When you were born, your parents didn't understand you. None of your siblings had ever been so difficult or so demanding. As an infant you cried for hours at a stretch and no one knew the reason. As a toddler you threw screaming fits and tantrums, as though you were tormented by your wishes. You didn't learn to speak till you were three years old and often wouldn't answer when a person spoke to you, although your ears were tested and your hearing found to be perfectly normal. You sometimes chafed against behavior when it was demanded of you. Always, you seemed strange and stubborn to your parents, and yet they loved you deeply, just as they loved all their children. Nothing mattered to them more than your well-being.

Your eldest sister, Sara, was in seventh grade when you were born. Your twin brothers, Matt and Finn, were ten years old. Maria, who was five, was the only small child in the house when your mother brought you home for the first time.

Being the baby of the family made you specially close to everyone and specially distant. For years you lived in different worlds. Your siblings played with you and tried to teach you. They picked you up and held you, took you to the park. They put you on the slide and pushed you on the swings. You were so cute, they always told you, hugging you tightly and kissing your face. Your hair was reddish-blonde and whether it was hot or cold outside, your cheeks were always pink.

When you were four, your parents ruled you like a king and queen. Everyone told you what to do. Your mother was a busy woman. Always, there were pressing chores she needed to accomplish. Important errands filled her head, and this was how she liked to live her life. She was shocked by people on park benches. She said she'd die if she were forced to sit that way in public, staring off in space and doing nothing. She was stern with herself and met her obligations. Always, she paid her bills on time, her house was clean, and her mind fixed on the welfare of the family. She set the table for your meals and cooked hearty food that people liked.

When you were five, you sat with everyone at dinner. Your family joined hands before they ate and offered thanks. Some nights, when your mother raised her head from grace and glanced at all your faces, she seemed to glow, like someone who'd been inundated by her blessings. As far as anyone could tell she never had been late for an appointment, she kept her promises, and was honest to a fault. She expected that her children, too, would be responsible and live what she'd have called "a decent life". Your father was the same, a soft-spoken history teacher, who did his best at everything he tried. Your mother said he was a gentleman, the finest she had ever met. It pleased you when he gazed admiringly at her, put his arm around her shoulder, or held her hand in his.

Your mother monitored her children closely, everything they did from table manners to hand writing to the way they greeted people on the street. You were expected to be pleasant company and thoughtful. There was no yelling in the house, no arguing or hitting. Your father cared about your speech and grammar. There was a proper way to say each sentence and each word. Many times he urged his children to speak clearly and more slowly. He couldn't understand you if you spoke too fast. While you were small, your mother liked to keep you occupied. You never dreamed how much you learned. It was beyond imagination.

You were important. Everything you did meant something. All people mattered just as much as you did. Everything mattered. Every tree and stone. It was the same with sun and earth, air and water; whatever you saw, felt, heard or smelled was able to exist for good or ill. If you lay in the sun too long, your skin would burn. If you stared directly at it, you'd go blind. You had to know how to drink water and not drown in water. How to survive the blazing heat of summer and the winter cold. How to enjoy a fresh breeze without fear and to prevail over a gale wind.

When you woke up each morning, you couldn't know how you would feel. Maybe because of a dream you'd had or a canker sore had suddenly appeared at the corner of your mouth and hurt. You might be hot or cold in bed, tired, nervous, numb, hopeful or excited by the feeling of the day. Outdoors, the weather never stayed the same, just as the moods which overcame you changed, as though you hadn't any say about your happiness or sadness, and your state of mind was chosen for you by the world.

Your clothing was important. It must be clean, not stained or ripped. Your shoes should not be scuffed or run down at the heels. Your socks needed to match. The zippers on your clothes must work and buttons on a shirt should not be missing. You needed to be clean from head to toe. Your teeth had to be cared for daily. All odors emanating from your body should be pleasing. Your fingernails and toenails must be clean and nicely trimmed.

❧ ❧ ❧

While you were young, your family noticed that your face was often serious. You smiled, but hardly ever laughed. There were many things that pained you. As always, you were full of longings and strong wishes, but your heart was soft. You apologized if you bumped into someone or stepped on a person's toe. No one had to urge you. It made you sad to see somebody hurt. A human being was so breakable, the skin so soft, it could easily be bruised or punctured deep enough to make somebody scream out loud. It could bleed and scar. You had to guard it and protect it.

Your parents watched you closely. Every look that crossed your face was an announcement and every movement of your body made a statement. Your tone of voice was not supposed to be surprising unless you'd been attacked or shocked by grief or pain or fear, or if you wanted to be funny. When your siblings were hysterical and fractured by a joke, you smiled and stared at them, sometimes with fascination, as though your thoughts were too complex to be confined to laughter.

Your family went to church on Sundays and took up an entire pew. The church was full. Row after row of people moved together. You kneeled and prayed in sync with everyone. You crossed yourselves, sat silently or stood up as a group in the enormous room. When you were six, you had a special singing voice and sang with perfect pitch. The more you knew the hymns, the louder you would sing them. At home your family sometimes sang together. Your father sat at the piano while you gathered side by side behind him. You sang song after song and harmonized until your voices made a blended cloud of sound. Each time you sang, your cheeks turned to a dark rose color, your eyes shone, and when a song was done, you smiled.

❧ ❧ ❧

Your family noticed how sensitive you were. When Sara left for college, you missed her presence in the house, and cried at night the first weeks she was gone. Also, your health was fragile. Your siblings weren't sick the way you were. Always, you were coming down with stomach viruses, head colds, and allergies. You never minded being in your bed with a high fever. Lying idle and half-conscious was a kind of freedom. Your sister, Maria, liked to read to you and was cheerful, yet your mother suffered every time you became ill. She hovered over you with medicines and foods, cold drinks and worried eyes till you recovered.

Your siblings often laughed at your strange questions. What would be wrong, you wondered, if you wanted to crawl instead of walk the four blocks down your quiet street to the playground? You wouldn't be hurting anyone, so what was wrong with it? What if you wanted to whistle while you walked the whole way backwards on the sidewalk? You knew you might be stopped by somebody and questioned. If you said you were doing it for fun, would someone ask you to please stop? Questions like these have always cropped up in your mind.

When your brothers became old enough to get a driver's license, they were so excited, they spoke of nothing else. Sometimes you rode with them while your father taught them driving on back roads. There were speed limits to watch and signs that ordered you to slow down or completely stop. Matt and Finn took turns behind the steering wheel. They had to learn how to accelerate and use the brakes. Also, to adjust the windshield wipers, the defroster, all the mirrors, headlights, turning signals, and how to read the blazing dials across the dashboard. Your family's car was long and shiny white. It was brand new without a single dent or scratch. One day, when he was practicing, Finn hit the brakes too suddenly and hard, throwing the rest of you forwards in your seats. You bumped your shoulder on the door, but nobody was hurt. Another day Matt turned onto a one-way street. Your father called a warning, while cars blared out their horns and people shouted at him on the sidewalk. The more you watched, the more you thought you'd never want to drive, though all your fears were needless. You'll never hit an animal or person with a car or have an accident. You are a careful driver.

When you were eight, your family spent a week in Maine for a vacation. Sara was with you, home for the summer. Your mother asked you to run next door and buy a loaf of bread, and handed you some money. As you went down Front Street in the little town, two women suddenly appeared before you, heading for the store you were approaching. They wore long skirts. From behind they looked as though they might be a normal mother and her daughter, but when they turned to hold the door for you, you saw that neither one of them had noses. At the center of each face was a round, dark hole below the eyes and just above their lips. You stared at them an instant and tried to hide the horror that ran through you. Inside the store you turned away, breath-taken. You kept your back to the women until you heard them leave. Moments later, when you stepped outside, you were relieved to find they'd disappeared. You ran quickly, holding the bread, and when you told your mother what you'd seen, she saw your startled eyes. "How terrible!" she cried. She threw her arms around you and rocked you side to side. You thought how many children must wail and shriek just at the sight of the two women, and the way some grown ups would stare cruelly at them with naked disgust.

"Maybe it's good at least they have each other," your mother whispered in your ear, kissing your cheek.

❧ ❧ ❧

When you were ten years old, a man drove through a red light and hit you with his car as you were crossing Farwell Street. He raced away as quickly as he could and left you bleeding and unconscious in the road. You have no memory of the accident, of people running towards you, the sound of sirens, or the shaft of sun that hit the road beside you. By the time the ambulance had reached the hospital, you were in a coma, so badly injured no one expected you'd survive. Your right leg was broken, one hip was badly shattered and your head was deeply gashed.

One by one your family members gathered in the hall outside your room, your mother shaking head to toe with terror, as though she'd never known that such an accident could happen. You lay expressionless, like a rock that never changed, and looked more helpless than an infant, encircled by beeping machines. Tubes of fluids poured into your body while nurses medicated you and watched your vital signs.

Your family took turns beside you. Often your mother sat by the end of your bed, her head bent forward, praying, as she held your feet, while Maria leaned her cheek against your sheets and touched your ankles. You never saw your family's faces, twisted up and paper-white, tear-stained, and desperate as they paced the halls while doctors came and went, expecting you to die.

For days you were encased in an unbroken silence more complete than any you had known, as you lay senseless, lost to all connection with the world. On your third afternoon in critical care, one doctor thought you wouldn't last another day, and yet that very night you felt a vague awareness deep inside you, a tiny pierce of longing which began at midnight. Every hour it grew stronger and more adamant, like a hunger. The need kept growing till it was so fierce, your mouth dropped open and you groaned. You heard your mother's voice and when your eyes came open, you saw your family's faces close above you, as though you had been given everything you wanted. It was a miracle, people said, the way you came back and recovered.

There was a piece of metal planted in your hip. Your broken leg was treated till it healed. After months of surgery and struggle, you began to walk quite normally. Soon, it was only when you exercised too long that you would start to limp, which still is true today. Sometimes you thought about the man who'd hit you with his car. Your parents always spoke of him with outrage and disgust, and the police would often say they were determined to track down the swine and see him punished. You listened to the fury and revulsion all around you, and yet the man appeared to be beyond your comprehension. When you thought of him you felt more fear than anger, as though something inhuman, like an arrow or a gun, had shot you down.

When you came home from rehabilitation, you were a quiet child. I'm sure you can remember it. You never felt more deeply loved by all your family, yet something huge had changed. Your mind seemed to be new, and your thoughts no longer felt familiar. Your parents saw that you were different. It was as though your final stubborn wish was to survive the accident, and after that you had become a passive person stripped of all desires. When the family sang at home, your singing voice was not so pure as it had been and not so forceful. It was as though you'd lost all passion along with the color in your cheeks, which now were permanently pale. As your birthday approached, you couldn't list a thing you wanted.

When you returned to school, you finished your assignments, but had no interest in your studies. You did not look miserable. You had a group of friends who welcomed you. Matt and Finn were turning into stars at basketball and soccer. Maria could draw anything so beautifully. You knew you'd never draw that way. You loved no special games, activities, or sports. In your free time you were happy to watch television, whatever show it was, or to lie resting on your bed, staring at the tree outside your window, a tree and bed you might have lost forever.

❧ ❧ ❧

Now you are nineteen, away at school. Some days, like everyone, you walk in such a dream across the campus, you see nothing that you pass. So much is taking place inside you, your concentration is entirely devoured. Other times you are humiliated by your mind, the way it judges everyone in sight. How foolish people look to you, how overweight they are, how awkwardly they move, how smug they seem, as if there is no end to all the flaws and vices you can see. On days like this you'll touch the scar on your left cheek that makes a jagged line across your face. You'll rub the scar, unknowingly, the way you do when your own thoughts are terrible to you, and find it a relief when you admire anything along the way, whether it's a plant or bird or person who uplifts you.

If only you could view yourself the way I do. You are not ugly. Your scar and limp are not the person that you are. When you are older, you'll forget the scar. For months on end it will not matter to you in the least. Yet if you think right now about your future, what fearful, twisted thoughts you have. You are, like all your classmates, so blind to everything that lies ahead. I wish to heaven you could clearly see all of the good that you will do. There is no question of it.

Some things about a person never change with time. Your kindness will stay with you all your life. Also, your perseverance. Right now you have no special interest or excitement as you study for exams and write your papers, and yet, from the sheer effort you put in, your grades are always high. Your intellect is a stove that has been stoked and stoked with driest, dusty wood, yet one day soon a spark will light your mind with such a fire that will illuminate the path to your life's work. Quite suddenly you'll feel that nothing matters to you more than what you can discover. A heightened color will flood back into your face.

✤ ✤ ✤

In two weeks you'll return to your hometown for Christmas. Sara lives alone with her young baby, Toby. She was divorced six months ago. Your father is now dead and gone two years. Your mother mourns for him, yet he is still so much a part of her, he's never left her.

The winter break from school will be a rest and a relief. When you see your family, they will be what you expect. You know each one so deeply, the shade and texture of each person's hair, as though you'd seen it magnified under bright light. Also, you've memorized the feel of all their hands, their arms and cheeks against you as you greet them. The scent of each of them will be familiar when you breathe it in.

Each time your family comes together as a group, you smile to see their faces all around you. It doesn't matter that you once were crippled by your father's disappearance. As you celebrate with meals and talk together, you will not feel the full extent of anyone's importance to you. You can't begin to sense life's greatest losses in advance. You may imagine them, but you will not be able to protect yourself or to prepare for family deaths.

✤ ✤ ✤

All people come to me for some small shred of certainty. Any is better than none at all. If only you could see how admirable you are. Have you heard the slightest scorn in what I've said to you today? I know too much for scorn. You are not a lost, pathetic, foolish person. Soon you will find your way. Someday you will be married, like Maria and your brothers. You'll have children of your own and love them more than you have ever loved yourself.

I see too much for you to ever see. All the clothes and shoes you wear in your whole life piled up together in a heap would make a pointed hill, like an Egyptian sculpture standing in a desert. All the shadows you have ever cast. A map of every fingerprint you've left behind. There's nothing I can't see.

Does anyone know you better than I do? Please try to think of this, my friend, far longer than you've thought of anything before.

Winter Scene

The kitchen was orderly and quiet. You could hear the steady hum of the refrigerator, and for a while there was no other sound. In the morning light the empty sinks and painted cupboards were intensely white. At nine a.m. the sun shone on the copper pot that hung above the stove and flashed in the metal toaster on the counter.

Four chairs were pushed up neatly to the round kitchen table at the center of which sat a red glass bowl. The only piece of fruit left in the bowl was a banana. It was a brilliant yellow with no black spots on it, still firm although it had been two days on the sunny table and three nights in the dark. Another day would turn it soft.

Outside the window was a winter scene. The square back yard was deep in snow. Birds came and went from the bird feeder. Wind swayed the pine trees, and the shadows of the waving trees moved back and forth over the shining surface of the kitchen floor. The window rattled sometimes in the wind, and when the wind blew hard, a draft came in over the table, till the skin of the banana grew quite chilled. Then the wind died out, and the dust motes slowed and settled in the lighted air.

At ten a.m. a black cat padded across the floor, making no noise at all until it stopped by its dishes to lap at the water and nibble the remaining food. Soon there were sounds outside, the cat's head jerked up, and it ran from the room just as the kitchen door flew open. A woman entered, and a burst of cold that whipped the kitchen air into a frenzy. The woman kicked the door shut with her toe. The table shuddered and the copper pot shook on the wall as she stomped across the floor, snow falling from her boots, carrying a grocery bag in each arm. She nearly dropped both heavy bags onto the table. "WHAH!" was the sound she made as she released the bags. Her purse slipped from her arm and fell to the floor with a small thud, but she swept down, grabbed the purse up, and hurried from the room, leaving a trail of snow across the floor. In a moment she was back with loafers on her feet. She'd taken off her gloves and coat. Now she began to put away the groceries. Many items went into the refrigerator and the rest into the cupboards she yanked open and snapped shut.

She piled the fresh fruits by the sink to wash. Then set a pan of water on the stove to boil. She switched the radio on, moved the dial from sound to sound until she found a marching band and let this stay. She turned the volume up, then crossed the room, picked up the glass bowl from the kitchen table, carried it over to the sink, removing the banana, which she placed with the other fruit. She scrubbed the bowl with soap and rinsed it with hot water. She dried it till it shone, and held it up to the light, so the deep red of the glass darkened her face. She washed two oranges, two apples, and two pears, and arranged them in the bowl, all glistening with water. The banana she didn't wash, but placed it on top of the other fruit. She wiped the kitchen table with a sponge, and put the fruit bowl, like a centerpiece, upon it.

The water on the stove was heating up, starting to steam. The radio band marched on. The woman disappeared out of the room, but came back in a flash carrying two coffee mugs and two wine glasses balanced on a large, crumb-covered plate. She set the dishes in the sink. Rinsing the plate first, she put a stopper over the drain, squirted out some dish soap, and turned both faucets on so that the water poured out slowly. She paused for an instant, staring down past her white blouse and the glint of her gold bracelet at the kitchen floor, which was puddled with melted snow. She reached into a tall closet, pulled out a mop, and moved with heavy steps across the room. Holding the mop in one hand, she opened the refrigerator with the other, retrieved a slice of white bread, and let the door swing shut. She peered at the steaming water in the pan, then popped the bread into the toaster, and pushed the lever down as far as it would go.

Both faucets were still running, foaming up the soap and water in the sink. The woman mopped the floor. She hummed with the marching radio and then began to sing the melody in a high voice, bumping the chairs as she passed by, butting the table with her thigh in such a way that shook the water drops poised on the fruit so that they broke loose and rolled off the apples and pears down into the red bowl. The shadows of the pine trees reared and swayed over the shining floor and shimmered up and down the back of her white blouse, like a wild massage that she could neither see nor feel as she leaned forward, mopping the melted snow with rhythmic strokes.

Quite suddenly the woman stopped. She jerked upright. Her eyes had become wide and staring. Her mouth dropped open, and she let out a small cry. The braceleted arm flew to her forehead as she lurched sideways, still holding the mop, and fell hard against one of the kitchen windows. The glass broke with a shattering sound that made all of the birds in the back yard fly up together from the ground and feeder. The woman groaned. She raised herself, and managed to stand straight before she toppled forward and collapsed with her arms outstretched across the table, knocking two chairs onto their sides, sending the fruit bowl skidding off the edge, its red glass smashing into bits.

The woman's body sank back on itself, like liquid streaming off the table, and hit the floor with a loud thud that made the copper pot up on the wall hop off its nail and clatter down onto the counter. There was a short click as the bread popped in the toaster, and the sharp smell of the toast was instantly dispersed and whipped away to nothing by the cold air that poured through the broken window. The woman lay on her left side. She was completely still. Only her hair was moved and gently lifted by the outdoor air that blew and circled past her.

The band ended its march, and in the room there was the sound of water furiously boiling, hissing at the sides of the hot pan, and dishes shifting in the sink, floating up or falling through the rising level of soap-covered water as it reached the top and poured from one sink over to the other

By one p.m. the sky was cloudy. There were no shadows on the kitchen floor. The cat stood in the doorway, sniffing the cold air that filled the room. The water on the stove had boiled away completely, and the blackened pan gave off a burnt, metallic smell. Outdoors, the birds were back, filling the yard and crowding to the feeder. Their cries came loudly through the broken window. The cat moved into the room warily. She kept her body low to the floor as she moved forward with crouched, furtive steps. Sometimes she stopped abruptly, nervous and staring, as she wove her way across the strew of glass, pieces of fruit, and fallen chairs until she reached the woman. With a quick, bobbing motion the cat sniffed the woman's face, moving her nose across the woman's cheek up to her forehead and into her hair. She sniffed carefully and deeply, as though she had become oblivious to the cold room, the sizzle on the stove, and the water overflowing in the sink. Then the kitchen telephone began to ring, the red hot pan upon the stove let out a loud, explosive CRACK, and the cat leapt up and bounded from the room.

A man was speaking on the radio. Out in the yard it had begun to snow. Some jarring sound or unexpected sight made all the birds fly up together from the ground in a dark crowd, and in an instant they had disappeared from view.

Bed Check

Marie Dunn was forty-two years old, a psychiatric nurse who worked the night shift at the V.A. hospital. During the week she arrived on the ward by ten p.m. to start the bed check. She walked down the long, lighted hallway, stopping at every doorway to shine her flashlight on each bed. She felt relieved to see how peaceful the men looked in their sleep with all the trouble gone, erased completely from their faces. Even the old ones looked serene and oddly young.

Albert Keyes was always wide-awake, waiting for her as he did each night. He was a bird-like, little man in his mid-sixties, round-eyed and painfully thin, who would speak to nobody but her. Often his pajama top was open. When she leaned down to button it, she was touched by the sight of his small chest that looked as smooth and bony as a boy's. She tucked in his sheets and sat down on the end of his bed. She couldn't remember how the ritual had started, but she always sat with Albert for a while before he went to sleep. She sat the same way every night, gazing at the open doorway, the light from the hall illuminating her large face and heavy body, while Albert watched her from the dark.

Marie was perfectly at ease sitting with Albert, the way she was with all the patients, no matter how confused or frightening they might seem to people on the outside. Overweight and a plain appearance had made her feel outcast all of her life, almost as much as if she had an illness. She lived alone with a small, white cat, and felt a sharp discomfort with most people. She had been hurt by cruel remarks about her looks. Young men and boys were usually the ones to say the brutal words. Girls and women stared at her in silence or quickly looked away. Most often out in public she was totally ignored, and yet some days she held her breath when she walked down a crowded street, as though she could expect a shower of hostility or ridicule at any moment. The hospital was a refuge for her, and each time she entered its glass doors, she was relieved.

It was odd how close she felt to Albert Keyes, who spent most of his days oblivious to everything about him, lost in a mind so overwhelmed that he sat frozen like a statue in his chair eight hours at a stretch unless somebody moved him. And yet he came to life each night while she was with him. A thousand times she'd asked herself why this was so. She'd seen the difference in him start just after Christmas, the way his face cleared when she entered the room. It was astonishing to see the change. His eyes became alert and focused, and he looked as though he'd been released from all his demons. Some nights he almost smiled, yet Marie sensed that it would strain him terribly were she to try to draw him into conversation. Even to look at him too long might be too much for him, she thought.

She'd told nobody yet about the change she'd seen in Albert, as though he'd dared to step out onto a dangerous high wire and a noisy audience might make him fall.

She'd read his charts and seen nothing reported. Once, she'd asked Ann Arthur, one of the day nurses, whether she'd noticed any difference in him. Ann shook her head, amazed that anyone would ask if Albert had improved.

Tonight, while Marie sat with him, he watched her so intently, she could feel the shine of his expression coming through the dark, surrounding her like heat. She was aware of his tension, how it built and built as he waited for the moment when she'd pat his leg and stand up from the bed.

"Good-night, Albert," she said at last. His head rose from the pillow, as it always did, his neck cords jutting out, both eyes fixed on her face.

"Good-night." The words came from his mouth in a toneless voice that never failed to move her. Some nights the happiness that cropped up in her chest made her face flush red. She paused outside of Albert's room, as though she needed to collect herself before she joined the other nurses. She stood in the hall with her hand up to her throat, filled with a sense of over-sized emotion. It was the way she felt some mornings coming home from work when she looked up and saw her white cat in the window, waiting for her. Star would jump onto her bed when she lay down and settle on the pillow, curling in a ball by Marie's head, and purring in her ear with a loud happiness that sounded total, as though the little animal had everything it wanted.

Once, in a crowded elevator and another time when her back tooth was being drilled, Marie was surprised to think of Albert Keyes. In the dentist's chair her mouth was stuffed so full of gauze, she was afraid that she might choke. The drilling went on minute after minute, the pain grew worse and worse, and her heart began to race. She closed her eyes, and she thought of Albert's face. She could see him perfectly clearly: his thinning hair, his ghost-white skin, the v-shape of his eyebrows, and the fine lines by his mouth. He was there before her, looking at her, and she kept her eyes fixed hard on his small, black eyes until the dentist stepped back and the drilling stopped.

These afternoons, when Marie put on her uniform and left for work, she could see the days were growing longer. The sky was noticeably brighter. Inside herself she also felt a change. As she walked up the steep hill to the hospital, she could never tell whether she'd be tense or relaxed with her co-workers on the ward. Some nights she barely spoke a word to anyone and felt almost invisible. People ignored her. Yet other times the nurses were more friendly than they'd ever been before. It was a mystery to her why this was so. "Hi, Marie," they'd say the moment she entered the day room. Sometimes they'd come up to her, pat her shoulder, even put an arm around her. As they approached, she never knew what she would do. If she felt uncomfortable, she'd make a quick excuse and hurry off. But there were times when she'd sit down with them, making a circle, and begin to talk without the slightest fear. They took turns, speaking of the hospital, the patients, or themselves. Some nights the words poured out of her, as though she'd been released from all her fierce self-consciousness and stiffness, and every barrier that stood between her and the women had been thrown down and tossed away. While Marie spoke, the color rose in her face. It was a paradise the way she felt talking to Jilly McCabe, Sue James, and Lillian Grunwald. Words flew from her mouth, and all the motions of her body gracefully flowed. Sometimes she let her head fall back. She laughed, like somebody completely normal, aware of the dizzy confusion and the spinning joy inside her head, as though she'd lost all sense of what she looked like in the world and who she was.

THE CRITIC

At seventy he was almost completely bald, a short man with a large paunch, who wore old bow ties, faded white shirts, and pants held up by dark suspenders. He had a beak-like nose that came to a sharp point, a thin line of a mouth, and dusky-colored cheeks shot through with broken veins. He drank heavily, both out in public and at home alone, and liked strong-smelling, fat cigars that felt enormous in his mouth.

His opinions were well known. He'd written books, newspaper pieces, and articles for magazines. He'd been seen on television, heard on radio, and had traveled widely, giving interviews and delivering speeches.

Anger made his mind work at its best. He was never more articulate than when he raged. The words that welled up in his brain hammered with power. He could feel how brilliant he became. He touched the truth with an electrifying ease. And he was wildly funny. Contempt unlocked all of the humor that was in him. When he held forth at parties, rooms filled with people crumbled and collapsed with laughter.

He loved sophisticated company, men and women just like him, who could be harsh and witty. Sometimes the top of his head would almost blow off with delight between the hurl of barbs and the resulting gales of laughter.

He was uncomfortable expressing admiration. Praise made him sound weak and simpering to himself, and insincere. Scorn raised him up until he felt supreme, like someone made of iron.

Sometimes he was half-startled by the force of his own mind, when the words that emanated from it had all the fury of a murderous explosive. By the time he'd finished there was little left of what he had attacked.

Once his anger was successfully expressed and done with, he felt diminished, the wind gone out of all his sails, as though he'd lost his fire and could only hope some new intense dislike would re-invigorate him. Sometimes his hatreds hid from him, like buried gold, and were as hard for him to find as an enduring love.

He'd had three marriages and been divorced two times. There were two children by his final wife, who seemed in competition to see which one could fail in life most grievously. His son of forty-four was grim-faced and depressive, prone to accidents, illness, and financial troubles. He'd never lasted longer than a year at any job. His daughter was a drug addict, who'd been in and out of hospitals for fifteen years. More than once she'd tried to kill herself, but managed to survive. He was not fond of his children and had little contact with them. The last time they'd been together in one room he'd told them how they'd disappointed him and shamed him. His wife, who was quiet, meek, and fearful of his anger, tried to stop him from yelling at the children. He'd rarely turned on her before, but on that one occasion he'd been harsh with her and scathing, as though he'd never realized how much he could dislike her until then.

"Are you so perfect?" his son had shouted at him. "Who are you to judge us anyway?" The truth was he'd no idea who he was. He'd never analyzed himself and had no intention ever to become self-reflective, no matter that his wife died of a massive stroke two days after he'd lashed out at her or that his children blamed him for their miserable lives. He didn't judge himself. He could watch his belly swell out like a beach ball without self-castigation. All his disapproval was directed, like gunfire, elsewhere. Sometimes he shot and shot, reloaded, aimed and shot till every shred of bile in him was gone.

He drank huge, soothing tanks of liquor every day, starting at noon. Then, after a nap, he looked forward to the long stretch of imbibement that started in the evening. He liked a dinner that had been preceded by rounds of chilled martinis.

When he went out socially, his face was blank, swept clean of all expression. Until he spoke it was impossible to know his mood or what he might be thinking. He'd reached a point of eminence where people treated him like royalty, and he took social liberties he'd never have dreamed of as a young man. Often he fell asleep in the middle of a dinner at somebody's house. His head nodded until his chin finally settled on his chest. He snored loudly while people carried on the meal around him. No one dared to wake him. Even while he slept, he appeared stony and invulnerable, like a walled fortress.

At a dinner party he went to one night the people laughed at everything he said. Waves of laughter swept the table with such force that nobody could eat. Each time they took a bite, he spoke, and once again their roaring shook the room till all the guests were weak and begging him to stop. That night he felt their laughter reaching out to him like arms. He was laughing, too, sometimes without control, like a machine whose switch was broken and could not be stopped. There was a moment when his whole face changed. He was still laughing, but his eyes turned red and brimmed with tears, as though the funny thought quite suddenly had turned sad. One woman at the table saw the change in him. There was a stunned expression on his face. Tears were rolling down his cheeks. As she looked across the table her mouth dropped slightly open and her breath stopped in her throat. By then all of the guests were staring at him. It was as if the table had been stripped completely bare and there was nothing on it: no plates of steaming food, salt shakers, candles, wine, or fragrant sauces.

"Are you all right?" someone managed to say. He didn't answer. The tears that wet his face were a response to the quick burst of wild, excruciating pain that had opened up inside him and was now concentrated in his chest, stabbing through him with a force that made him gasp as he rocked back and forth, his hands clutching wildly at himself, his head bent low, like someone being bludgeoned. In all his life he'd never felt such unrelenting, dreadful pain. On and on it went, like someone screaming. He slid from his chair to the floor and rolled onto his side, writhing. His eyes were shut, his whole self trapped in pounding anguish. Beneath it all some small part of his mind was watching closely, taking note of everything that happened. This was the end of him, he was thinking. He knew it with the certainty of someone who had leapt from a high cliff and now was flying towards the ground. As he rolled onto his back with a loud moan, he could feel how frightening his own body had become to him.

Looking up, he saw people above him, crowding over him and staring down with eyes that mirrored his own terror. Their legs were inches from his face, and yet he might have been a thousand miles away, flung out into some arctic, empty space where nobody could reach him. A brown-haired woman in a shimmering, red dress lowered herself until she was kneeling close beside him. She was speaking to him, but he couldn't hear her or answer. All the air was leaving him. He couldn't get his breath. He saw himself, his giant wreckage lying on the floor, as though he were seeing everything from far above. He watched the woman touch his huge, protruding stomach, saw his dreadful-looking face flung back, the dark blood vessels broken in his cheeks, his cruel, little mouth, all so ugly to him that it seemed astounding she would even touch him. Yet she was gently lifting his bald head. She was opening his frightful mouth. He could see her face so clearly, the gravity of her expression, the determination in her eyes, and the red-lipped mouth she brought down tightly over his as she began to breathe into him carefully and strongly and steadfastly, as though he were something hugely valuable and precious that needed to be saved.

THE PENANCE

1.

The man with the bruised arm and the woman with the blackened eye were silent as they rode down in the elevator, though their minds were racing and the urge to speak was strong in both of them. But they had made a pact, and part of it was that they would remain silent for the day. Not a word would they speak, no matter what happened to them in the next twelve hours. They had decided this with little discussion, as if they realized that what they'd done was far too serious for words, and nothing they could say would heal the damage.

Already it was harder for the woman to be quiet than the man. She was used to talking freely and had a need to empty herself quickly of everything important that came into her head, as though her mind was a small space that always threatened to be cluttered and her most pressing thoughts were refuse that must be continually thrown out.

The man had an aversion to self-analysis and was not used to dwelling on his feelings, but as he rode down in the elevator, he could not deny the fear lodged in his stomach that fanned to life with every breath he took. It would not go away.

They had been married for three years, and though there had been spats and disagreements, they had never had a serious argument in all that time. Yet last night over something trivial and foolish they had turned on each other and fought with an anger that only seemed to grow more adamant and loud until the woman smashed a plate to bits against the kitchen sink, and grabbing her arm, her husband slapped her face. Now, when they looked back, the memory of the night was overwhelming. The ugly words they'd shouted remained with them like the shards of glass that even now lay strewn across their kitchen floor.

In the elevator they stood side by side. The woman was twenty-nine and the man had just turned thirty, but they looked younger than their years. Although their eyes were downcast and their expressions somber, their faces had the vacancy of youth and showed no permanent reaction to the world. They were holding hands. This, too, was part of their agreement. That they would hold hands all day long, whether they wanted to or not. Already their hands were unpleasantly warm. The man had begun to perspire, as though the high humidity of the sweltering city had so invaded the air-conditioned building that the touch of a human hand was all it took to make him sweat. Yet as the elevator landed and the doors slid open, he grasped the woman's hand more tightly, as though he was afraid she might let go.

They paused at the glass entrance door, and for an instant their minds were like twin landscapes reflecting the same view. The city street they saw shone in a fierce, yellow light, and they had to gird themselves before they stepped outside. It was 8 a.m. and the heat was poisonous already. The night had never really cooled the air at all, and the woman felt half-faint as they started up the sidewalk. They'd had no breakfast and they'd hardly slept last night. The man had fallen on their bed and the woman sprawled across the couch. They'd slept five hours before they woke up in their clothes, the same clothes they were wearing now. The woman glanced down at her wrinkled blouse. There was a brown spot on the collar the size of a dime that looked like dried blood. Her skirt was badly creased, and as she thought of her appearance, her eye began to throb. She'd seen it briefly in the hall mirror, puffed and blackened all around, and now she wished she'd thought to wear sunglasses. Never had she gone out in public in such disarray. Her face was without make-up and her hair uncombed, and as she realized how dreadful she must look, she felt as unprotected and alarmed as if she'd suddenly been thrown out on a stage before a staring crowd. It was a Wednesday morning and the street was filled with people hurrying to work, the men with hair slicked back, briefcases swinging, and everyone clean-looking in fresh clothes. As each person approached, the woman lowered her eyes and prayed it wouldn't be someone she knew. It was horrifying how conspicuous she felt, and she was overwhelmed to think that anyone should see her like this, so much that she could concentrate on little else. Her appearance suddenly meant everything to her, was the most important thing in the world, and to go on like this for one more minute was more than she could bear. She was about to wrench her hand away and run back to the building, but when she looked up at her husband, she was not prepared to see his face so wretched. His eyes burned with pain, as though the memory of last night entirely consumed him, and the sight of his suffering struck her heart with such a force, it was as if the sidewalks had been suddenly swept bare of everyone but them. She squeezed his hand consolingly. In an instant all her longing to turn back had disappeared, and for a while she walked ahead so cloaked in thoughts of him and his distress, she felt invisible to everything they passed.

❧ ❧ ❧

Under the grilling light that seemed to pound the street and everything about them, the man was feeling ill. Waves of nausea rose to his constricted throat. As they approached the boulevard, his head was aching, and he found it hard to imagine how they would endure the heat or manage to survive this day at all. He asked himself if they weren't mad to do what they were doing. The plan they'd made was that they'd walk for hours, taking no food or drink. They would not stop to rest. They were to walk the whole way to Heath Station, which was at the heart of the most dangerous part of the city, a place they'd never been to. Heath was notorious for its violence, and its crimes were heavily reported in the news. Stories of robberies, gangs-wars and murders in that twelve block area were constant. The man and woman planned to walk through Heath, and if they were attacked, they had agreed that they would offer no resistance. They wouldn't raise a hand to defend themselves and would accept whatever happened to them as if it were their due. They had set down all of their rules in the early light of dawn as they sat side by side, white-faced and sickened by their own behavior. And for that brief period while they'd planned this day, they'd been stripped of all emotion, cool and calm-voiced, and so perfectly attuned, it seemed they shared a single mind. Each had accepted the suggestions of the other, and in the space of a few moments they had laid out a scenario that became as structured and demanding as a play. If they arrived safely at Heath Station, they would continue on into the final act. They would ride the train back home, remaining silent all the way, no matter how tired or relieved or exuberant they might find themselves to be. And once they'd reached their building, they would still say nothing to each other. They would allow themselves a drink of water, but they would eat no dinner. And when they fell into their bed to sleep it was their hope that this day would remain unforgettable and monumental in their lives, like a great wall of protection they had built against all future violence between them.

Lack of sleep and food and the extreme heat had made the man already feel a stranger to himself, yet as they stood under the baking light, waiting to cross the boulevard that flashed with moving vehicles, he was half-appalled to find that he and the woman at his side had stepped so far out of their normal lives and were now actually undertaking what they'd planned. His throbbing head and the rhythmic pulse of nausea in his throat were like repeated signals warning him to turn back. But when the lights changed and the traffic stopped and parted, he moved forward instantly with the gathered crowd of people that swept across the open space in a great wave. Once on the other side, he was propelled ahead like someone caught up in a current stronger than his body or his will, and as he thought of what they'd planned, there was admiration mingled with his fear, the way a man can waken from a nightmare to find himself both chilled and awed by the inventive power of his mind. As he led his wife out of the crowd around a sudden corner and onto an unfamiliar street, he felt unpleasantly alive, as though they'd entered a new realm where all of their experience would be potent.

❧❧ ❧❧ ❧❧

They'd barely left their neighborhood behind, yet it seemed to the woman they had already walked for hours. The smoky, yellow air that hung about them was heavy with the smells of car exhaust and garbage. She kept sniffing at it, searching for some current of freshness, but every inch of air seemed to be sullied by an odor. And there was no charm to anything she saw. She cast her eyes about, but everything in sight looked soiled and ugly in the wilting heat, like a reflection of herself. The more she thought of it, the more it seemed the punishment they'd chosen for themselves was unnatural and excessive. No one they knew would do what they were doing, she was sure. Walking to Heath Station was as reckless and unhinged as the fighting they had done, and it frightened her to think that their behavior was abnormal. Yet she could not forget the closeness, the overwhelming oneness they had felt as they had planned this day, as if the extremity of their situation had pushed them to some new level of intimacy. Their plan, which seemed to come to both of them at once from out of nowhere, was like a complex thought already formed that only needed them to put it into words. She remembered the conviction with which they'd set down all their terms and the way they'd looked into each other's eyes, almost with pride, when they had finished, as if their penance had already been accomplished because they had conceived of it so well. The more the woman thought, the more confused she grew. She was so used to airing all her feelings, and she liked to solve a problem as she spoke of it out loud. Questions that seemed unanswerable and immense could be reduced to comforting simplicity when they were dismantled by her ordinary voice. Even the darkest thought could lose its power to disturb her once it was expressed. To be so locked in quiet was a kind of torture to her, and yet, she told herself, it had been she who had suggested that they spend this day in silence.

A picture of their cool, darkened apartment filled

her mind. She saw herself sweeping the glass up from the kitchen floor, washing the pile of dishes they'd left in the sink, wiping the counters, feeling the calm descend upon the room as it grew clean. Then moving to the bedroom, straightening the rumpled spread till it was smooth across their bed, pulling the shades against the heat and sun, the sound of traffic coming up from a great distance far below. She thought of how she'd carefully dust and vacuum all the rooms, as though each speck of dirt had been a witness to her shame. She imagined the relief of stripping off her soiled and sweaty clothes, the stained, white blouse she'd never wear again. The moment she removed it, she would throw it in the trash along with all the clothes that she was wearing. The more she thought of going home, the more she fixed on it. If she begged her husband to turn back, she wondered what he'd say. Before last night she'd have been able to appeal to him so easily. Her slightest wish would have been paramount to him. But there was a harsh determination in his face that she had never seen before, as though the night had changed him. She felt she could no longer guess what he was thinking. The hand that held hers was the hand of someone who had hit her, and as she focused on the pain around her eye, remembering the fury of the blow he'd given her, she felt her heart turn hard against him. All of her insides seemed to flame with renewed anger till she could taste the poison of it in her mouth. And yet she didn't *want* to hate him. Not at all.

As though some message of her turmoil had passed down her arm and from her body over to his, her husband gently squeezed her hand. At the affection of his touch, tears sprang to her eyes. The sidewalks and the buildings swam together in a blur of light that seemed to match the jumbled shift of feelings that went on within her.

❦ ❦ ❦

The man was feeling sicker by the moment. His face had lost all of its color, and there was a ringing in his ears that grew louder and louder, as though some cataclysmic sound were fast approaching that would soon engulf him. He raised his eyes up to the sky for some relief, but the yellow air that rose for miles above was like a suffocating broth so thick with substances that he could actually see the hard, white particles that swirled and shone within it. Each breath he took increased his nausea. His stomach had always been delicate to stress, especially in matters that pertained to love. The night at dinner in a restaurant when he'd worked up courage to propose marriage to his wife, he'd had to leave the table before she'd given him her answer, and rushed through a haze of candlelight to the men's room where he'd been violently ill. Now he was quite sure that he would have to stop and vomit right here on the pavement. He *wanted* to be sick, but was afraid of what his wife's response would be. He could imagine her cry of concern and the blurt of heedless words that would pour out, shattering the quiet that had built like a fragile bond between them. It was ridiculous how much he dreaded the thought of her speaking, as though all of the future hung on their present behavior, and their smallest actions had become so crucial that he would rather choke on his own vomit than let himself be sick. But after ten more steps, he had no choice. He stopped suddenly, and looking sharply at his wife, he put a finger to his lips in a signal of silence before he bent forward over the gutter, still holding her hand, and threw up with a gasping speed until he brought up nothing but dry heaves. The moment he was finished, he raised his head and started walking briskly forward, making it clear that he had no intention but to continue on their way. His breathing was uneven and there was a bitter taste left in his mouth, but already his head had cleared. The ringing in his ears was gone, and though his legs felt oddly light and a chill passed through him even while his forehead was beaded with sweat, he felt remarkably improved, stronger than he'd been all morning, and able to think. His wife walked quietly beside him, matching her steps to his, so that their bodies seemed to move in perfect unison, and for a moment he was overcome with a wild sense of gratitude, as if they'd met the challenge of a great ordeal.

The treeless, cobbled street that sloped away before them shimmered in the heat. It was an old street of ramshackle, wooden buildings, and after the crowded boulevard, it looked abandoned. For a while there were no people in sight. They were descending from the highest elevation of the city, and the view below them on all sides was veiled in smog. In the distance they could see nothing but a crowd of high-rise buildings, pale and spectral-looking through the haze, and the fierce glint of an unknown church spire. The man moved confidently forward. He'd always counted on his good sense of direction, and in his mind was a clear map of the whole city, although he hadn't been to half the places in it. He knew what neighborhoods they'd have to cross and that the remainder of their walk would be entirely down hill. The farther down they went, the worse the neighborhoods would grow, and they would find Heath waiting at the very bottom, smoldering and buried under all the layers of the city's air.

❦ ❦ ❦

The woman didn't try to think of autumn and the heaven of coolness that would cut through this misery of heat. She didn't think of comforts or of their apartment any longer. Although she couldn't trace the moment it had happened, she had reached a turning point that told her she must go the whole way to Heath Station with no deviation from their plan. It was as if she had re-captured the full meaning of this day with such a fervor that left no conflict in her. Only dismay at her short-sightedness and weakness. For she could now imagine the sense of failure and betrayal and the loneliness that would have assailed her had she left her husband on the road and returned to their apartment on her own. And with a steely certainty she knew there could be no moment free of pain till they had overcome the memory of last night, which was again so sharp and so alive in her whole body that every cell within her seemed to cry out with regret. Vaguely, she was aware of her feet. The new black flats she wore were not the proper shoes for walking. She could feel the pebbles and the grit that had collected in them. Her toes were pinched, as though her feet had swelled, and her right heel hurt with every step she took, like a shrill note added to the symphony of her discomfort. By the time this day was over she was sure the heel would be rubbed raw. She imagined it, swollen and bleeding, and her husband's look of wonder when he realized how bravely she had suffered.

Now everything had become simple. The miles to Heath were like a long, dark tunnel they had entered from which there was no possibility of escape. All they could do was to proceed forward, step by step, until they reached the end. There was no longer any need to think, the woman told herself, and yet her mind continued on, no matter how she wanted it to rest.

❧ ❧ ❧

Since they'd begun their walk, the man had checked his wrist repeatedly and been surprised each time to find his watch was gone. He'd left it back at the apartment on the table by their bed. Last night, during the havoc of their fight, he'd smashed the crystal, though he had no memory of how he'd done it. The minute hand was bent up at an angle and the time had stopped at 1:05 a.m.. The watch was his most prized possession. It was a German watch of heavy gold, solid and distinctive-looking, an emblem of an earlier era when things were better made and meant to last. The watch had been his father's watch, and he had worn it for the past four years and developed an attachment to it that was almost superstitious.

Again he looked at his bare wrist. There was a jeweler across the street from his office building, and tomorrow, first thing in the morning, he would leave the watch to be repaired. He felt some small relief the moment he had made this plan. Though, as he thought of it, tomorrow seemed as far away as if a year must pass before it came. Without his watch the time had slowed so much he seemed to trudge through it like heavy mud, and felt the passing of each second. Every step he took was a single beat on a clock, and by the time he'd counted sixty steps, a minute had become immensely long. The hours that lay ahead appeared interminable, and he began to think this day would be the longest day he'd ever lived.

The sun was hidden in the haze, but the man could see that it had risen higher than he had expected. He guessed it must be after ten o'clock. He and his wife had left their cell phones back at the apartment, having agreed that they would not call their offices today. There would be no explanations or excuses for their absence till tomorrow, and they'd have to face whatever consequences this would cause. The man was thinking of the bustle of his office at this hour. On an ordinary day he arrived at work by nine. He was known to be responsible and prompt, and on those rare occasions when he thought he might be late, he always phoned ahead. By now his secretary would be worried. Probably she had already tried to reach him more than once at home. He could see the puzzled look on her young face and the frown that would appear as people asked for him. Today he would be absent from a staff luncheon he was expected to attend, and he realized with a jolt that he would also miss a meeting with an important client, an appointment made more than a month ago that it was inexcusable for him to miss. As the repercussions of his absence multiplied before him, the man was filled with agitation and annoyance. It had been his suggestion that they not call their offices today, and yet he blamed his wife for the idea. His devotion to his work and the long hours he put in had always been a major source of friction in their marriage and the cause of her most bitter complaints. He could see that in the misery of this morning he had wanted to placate her and prove to her that she was more important to him than his work. Yet now he felt as if she'd triumphed over him and trapped him into doing something he regretted. Her job was such that she was her own boss and this lost day would put her in no jeopardy. It might even go entirely unnoticed, because she often did her work at home. But his unexplained absence would be perceived as something shocking. It would be mentioned and discussed by everyone in his department. The more he thought of it, the more it seemed this day would be a lasting blight on him, a question mark about his character that no one would forget.

Out of the corner of his eye he was aware of his wife's form moving beside him. She was limping slightly, as though she'd hurt her foot, but he would not allow himself to look directly at her or to feel the sympathy that threatened to undo his irritation. His teeth were clenched, and as he moved forward through the wall of unremitting heat, he focused fiercely on the view before him. There were people swarming at an intersection far below. He watched their bodies gathering and swelling in dark masses at the four corners and saw them crossing towards each other like small armies

⁂ ⁂ ⁂

The woman breathed in the foul air willingly and gave herself up to the heat until she seemed to float above her body and its pain. The city sounds grew far away and indistinct, and superimposed on the brick sidewalk in the steamy light rebounding from the street, she saw her parents' farm as it had looked when she was a young girl. She saw the tall, white house in summer, the hollyhocks outside the kitchen, the woodpile neatly stacked beside the shed. Beyond the barn her father's fields of corn stretched all the way out to the dark line of the woods that circled the horizon like a fortress.

For the second time since they'd begun their walk, the man and woman came to a full stop. They'd reached the intersection and were waiting for the light to let them cross. The woman felt the press of bodies closing in around her and the granite weight that settled on her legs the moment she stood still, as though she couldn't possibly continue forward. But when her husband tugged her hand, she followed him without a pause, her ears full of the chatter of voices around her, her eyes fixed on the faces flooding towards her. Yet all the while she clung to the vision of her childhood house, which had come out of nowhere for no reason that she knew and rose before her in a kind of panoramic splendor. All she wanted was to disappear into the scene and to remember it more deeply. But her mind had skipped ahead, and now her thoughts were of her family, what they would think were they to see her hobbling down this ugly city street, in stained and wrinkled clothes, her hair matted and tangled, her eye so hideously swollen that she could barely see. She could imagine their anxiety and horror at the sight of her, the way they'd stare at her as if she had become a stranger to them, someone inexplicable. And there *was* no explanation she could give that would make sense to them. No way to tell them she was following an instinct like a thread, yet every step she took felt right to her, the way a mother wouldn't hesitate to run across thin ice to save her drowning child, but would rush headlong into danger, as though she'd suddenly been freed of every fear but one.

❦ ❦ ❦

At the intersection, when they walked right past Hardigan station, the man was surprised to realize how far they'd come. Heath was no more than four miles from them now, and he could feel some hint of pride at their accomplishment. His thoughts turned to his wife, like a returning soldier dreaming of his home, and for the first time since they had begun their walk, he looked directly at her. His breath caught when he saw her eye. Swollen blue and glaring in the light, it shone at him like a rebuke. And his wife was not the jaunty woman he'd imagined at his side. Strands of her hair hung limply by her face, and she looked dazed, frightfully pale and worn, as though she'd aged ten years in the past twelve hours. He couldn't bear to look at her and turned away. As he walked ahead, he tried to overcome the picture of her face and to remember how she'd always looked to him. He was holding her hand tightly in his own, and yet he missed her.

꽃 꽃 꽃

The woman did not know how far they'd come or how many miles still lay before them. Her only proof that they'd progressed was the deterioration that she saw around her. The little shops they passed were failing and decrepit. The painted signs above the doors were chipped and rusted, the wooden doorsills worn away, the windows smudged, as though the owners were resigned to ruin. And she could see a difference in the hard-faced people on the street, the women who stared sullenly at her and the men who eyed her coldly. There was hostility and strangeness in the cooking smells that came from the dark cafeterias and dingy little food shops and the driving beat of unfamiliar music that seemed to pass right through her body as it blared from cars and escaped from open doors and windows. They passed a trash-strewn little park where men lay motionless on broken benches in the baking sun. The smell of urine wafted out of alleys. Ahead of them the sidewalk shone with broken glass, like a preview of the greater devastation that was soon to come. Through all of this the woman walked quite numbly, distracted by the world of her own body. The pain she had successfully ignored for miles had come back with a searing urgency. Her feet were anguished. Every step she took was torment, and she had never been so blindly tired. She felt more and more light-headed, as though the air had lost its oxygen. No matter how deeply she inhaled, she still was short of breath. Her legs began to tremble, and she could feel the rhythm of her heart intensify in panic at the thought that she might suddenly collapse. She forced herself to take deep breaths, and staring grimly at the street, she willed herself to remain conscious.

❊ ❊ ❊

The walls of Wexford Station were blackened with graffiti, and as they passed it by, the man noticed a row of men, who stood like sentinels before the entrance and looked at him appraisingly, knowing he was an outsider to this part of town. He wished he'd worn blue jeans and that his wife was dressed more casually. While he'd left behind his tie and jacket, he was wearing a white business shirt, dress pants, his good belt, and a fine pair of leather shoes that had not lost their shine in spite of the long walk. From the pocket of his shirt protruded a gold pen, a gift from his wife last Christmas. As he thought of it, he pulled the pen out and slipped it into his pant's pocket, remembering that he'd had the sense at least to leave his wallet back at the apartment, and carried with him only money enough to cover their train fare home. The Wexford neighborhood was the roughest they had seen, and the atmosphere appeared to grow more threatening by the minute. A group of teen-aged boys was coming towards them up the street, swaggering and shouting at each other. He didn't have to look at her to know that his wife wore earrings and the gold pendant she was rarely without. Glancing down, he noted the bracelet on her wrist and felt under his finger the hard bulge of the diamond solitaire he'd given her for their engagement. His stomach tightened as he watched the mob of boys, and it seemed miraculously lucky when the loud group turned down a side road and disappeared from view. The man and woman passed a row of housing projects where the tallest windows caught the burning light. Women sat, as though immobilized, on the front stoops with listless children at their sides or by their feet. The man could sense that he and his wife drew constant attention. He kept his face averted from everyone they passed, ignoring muttered words and half-heard phrases, not knowing whether they were meant for him or not. All of his effort went into maintaining an appearance of composure before the eyes that seemed to burn into his flesh. They passed a knot of men that spilled out of a store and stood unmoving on the sidewalk, so that the couple was forced to step off of the curb to pass around them. A hush fell over the whole street. The man could feel his breathing grow more and more shallow until he hardly seemed to breath at all, and it was at that moment that his wife let out a cry, as though someone had struck her. Her hand jerked out of his, and she sank to the ground so quickly that he couldn't catch her.

2.

They lay entwined together in the air-conditioned train, the coolness like a salve against their over-heated skin. The man's arm was around his wife's shoulder. His face was buried in her hair. There was no one but them inside the car. The woman had kicked off her shoes. From where she lay, half-slumped across the seat, her legs drawn up beneath her, she watched the roof tops and tree branches that spun by the window. The furnace of the world seemed far removed from them, and they were headed back to everything familiar. What a paradise it seemed to think of their front hall, their quiet dinners, and all their normal habits, as though the life they'd led before last night had happened long ago and she could remember nothing but its sweetness. She held one of her husband's hands in both of hers and felt his breathing in her hair. Now that she lay so still, her body seemed to be entirely free of pain. Fatigue was her only discomfort. She sighed and closed her eyes to a confusion of images that whirled before her with a power that made it seem more restful not to sleep. As she gazed out the window at the passing view, she thought with long-ing of the sound of her own voice, the way her over-loaded head would empty, and as her words poured out, the world would become harmless again and perfectly clear, like a still lake after a storm, where she could see right to the bottom. She wanted to speak now to her husband, to rid herself of the last shadow that was in her. It was ridiculous. No one could blame her for faint-ing, and yet she felt that she had failed him.

⁂ ⁂ ⁂

Behind closed eyelids the man lay in a swoon. It was as if he could not stop walking and still moved to the rhythm of his feet. One foot followed another, and he was back out on the street, bathed in the ugly light and breathless in the heat, continuing on the way to Heath, as though he could not rest until they had arrived there. The train stations were passing, one by one, and very soon, he told himself, he'd have to raise his head to check their bearings. But he didn't want his concentra-tion to be broken yet. Their walk flooded his conscious-ness and loomed in his mind with an immensity that gave him comfort. He was remembering the moment when his wife lay unconscious on the ground before him, as though that vivid moment had already turned into a fantasy. He was imagining the spectacle they must have made before the crowd that watched; how he'd dropped down beside her on one knee into a position that was almost courtly and called her name with all the anguish of an actor at the height of a performance. But his emotion had been real. He was remembering how the harsh atmosphere of the street suddenly changed and softened, how the light that fell on everything lost its glare and became gentle and the fierce heat lifted and was gone, as though his cries of "MOLLY!" "MOLLY!"

had overturned and shaken the entire world around him. He'd lifted his wife and carried her in his arms, oblivious to the dramatic scene they made, calling her name in that same ragged voice that made the hard-eyed women on the stoops look up at him as though they'd been electrified with sympathy and ardor. The men had stepped back gracefully to let him pass, like comrades, and with the grandeur of a prince he'd carried his wife effortlessly, as though he'd never been so physically strong, keeping his eyes fixed on her, watching the faint rise and fall of her breathing with such concentration that the distance to Wexford Station disappeared in a quick flash. He'd found the row of men still standing by the entrance, and sailed right past them with the indifference of someone who'd become untouchable. He'd stopped beside a rusty water fountain, set his wife down gently on the ground, and cupping the water in his hands, he'd bathed her face and neck. When her eyes opened, he'd poured water in her mouth, watching as if it were the one thing in the world that mattered while the awful pallor faded and the color flowered in her face, until she seemed totally revived. Then, like somebody startled from a trance, he'd leaned down and drunk deeply himself, taking the water in great gulps.

Now, as he held his wife with his face lost in her hair, the man could feel all of the distance he had travelled just to reach her. Her head nestled on his chest, fit perfectly beneath his chin, and their bodies merged together like the pieces of a puzzle that had fallen into place. He held her without opening his eyes or moving, as though by doing so he could preserve each atom of their closeness. The train kept stopping at new stations. It slowed, came to a halt, the doors opened, they slammed shut. Then they were off again, gathering speed, the car rattling and shaking, as though it longed to jar them from this present moment, to have them see with their own eyes the roar of time outside the window, as it devoured the scenery, tore trees and buildings from them and sent them flying to the past, and hurled the future at them with such force that if they looked, he knew they would see nothing clearly anymore, only their faint reflections in the glass against a world that had become unrecognizable, as though it had expelled them.

PERFECTION

If it were possible, I'd lead you out of this room to another room or similar moment. Above a quiet meal, beside a candle, I'd have you repeat what you were saying. Your idea was so beautifully put, it took my breath away. But Polly wouldn't let you finish. She interrupted you at nearly every word and fractured the spell you almost cast till I could barely preserve your portrait of a native (was it South African?) who when he looked at a tree, looked at it differently than we do. For him an ugly tree did not exist, you said. All trees, no matter what they looked like, whatever their age or size, were perfect, just as all things were to him perfect creations. I saw him standing on a perfect hill under a perfect sky looking out of a perfect body at a perfect view, never saying to a friend, "Oh, what a beautiful tree," and I had a violent longing to silence Polly, who talks so much she never hears, who if she were a Christian and Christ himself appeared, would argue with him about church doctrine without a bit of awe. Tonight she is as annoying as a toothache. The evening is galloping on and you are about to leave the table.

Why haven't you gone already? I may never know. You and I always settle for the surface, like people who think a poem is destroyed if it is dissected or discussed too much, though I've never understood people like that, how, worshipping mystery, they can ever marry or want to follow any subject to the end, when they seem to believe that the truth on close inspection is always disappointing. But my own mind is contradictory. Right now, for instance, what if you were to urge me, though we aren't lovers or close friends, to sit on the bench beside you with my head resting on your shoulder? I can imagine it so well. Very softly, I'd say in your ear, "If all the clothes I change and wear and wash, if everything I do passes through my conscious sieve, leaving a residue later called memory, and all is changing and nothing predictable, how absurd it must be to ask me my opinion; my opinion of my mother, or the weather, or anything which, having known it, I would have loved, disliked, or held as many opinions as there are words. And if I must accept that my judgment will always be faulty, is it any wonder I wanted to cling to your vision of a native looking at a tree, who while I can't comprehend him, must seem like a super-human seer?" Barely knowing you, is it conceivable that I could reach across and gently touch your cheek? Just because it would be perfection, which may be like a passing wish for men and women like us.

I wonder why people ever speak at all, when everything they say is barely an outline, not even a précis, and no one is interesting or important enough to hold any audience for long. But what if you could never have enough of me? Or what if a man sat with a woman looking alert yet so relaxed it seemed he had no house to go home to, no job and no future demands at all? What if he said, "Tell me what you think about things," settled back without even a taste of food or drink to separate them? She, nonplussed, seeing he really might be serious, could fall completely mute, as though she had been handed a loud microphone, unable to believe he could really want to know. After all, what was so important about her lifetime? And if neither of them had a sex or any vanity, would they even bother to say hello as they passed each other on the street? But putting all of this aside, burdened with a sudden ton of experience and a chance to exist, she might half-laughing, maybe slightly embarrassed but mustering up her dignity, begin to speak. At first, with gratitude, she would keep her sentences short, and there would be no digressions. She would try to please, her tone of voice lively, embellished with graceful faces and gestures, pausing politely at the end of each clipped paragraph to wait for some encouragement. But each time, if she found him still fascinated, she might be tempted to say, "I think I'll tell you a long, involved story," just to test him. And if his eyes hadn't wandered from her face and his brain had turned into a boat whose movements she could direct, then she could go on. Turning to the third person, more dignified and refreshing than a continuous "I", and changing the sex of her protagonist for added interest, she would begin her tale.

"Once I had a friend who knew exactly what he wanted. When he was twenty-two, he took me for a drive one day to show me his dream house. If I never own it, I'll never be happy, he said. But he didn't appear to be gloomy, even though the young couple who owned the place had several children, dogs and cats, and appeared to be settled down to a long life in the vine-covered cottage. I've told them what the house means to me, he said as we drove off. And they've promised to contact me if they ever decide to sell.

When he was twenty-eight, my friend still gave himself good odds for happiness in spite of his unbending demands and rigid needs. He had a job that was satisfying to him. He had friends. He still did not own his dream house, but he had a large inheritance. If the house went up for sale, he'd not only be able to buy it, but to furnish it as well, exactly to the plan he would draw up for every room. But all of this is superfluous, he said to me. The thing that haunts me is the woman I want to marry. I haven't found her yet, though I know just what she looks like and how she dresses. I can hear her voice, what the tone of it would be, he said. I know I'll recognize her the moment I see her.

When I said to my friend, as I often did, that I thought he was cracked, probably the craziest person I'd ever known, he smiled. But to change my taste would be like trying to change the shape of my head or the length of my arms, wouldn't it? he asked. He was desperate. His affairs with women had been infrequent and unsatisfying. That he had never been in love tormented him. Yet his pursuit of his fantasy lady, who stood in the way of all others, continued, and became more frantic every year, until it was evident to his friends that he was no longer a charming eccentric but a neurotic whose obsession needed a psychiatric cure. He submitted to the advice of everyone he knew, but after four years of therapy, his dream was still intact, and he resumed the search for his wife with a determination that was more grim than ever.

Here, at the apex of her story, the woman might pause to catch her breath, wait for more encouragement or to luxuriate a bit before relinquishing her spell. And her snared listener, nettled and impatient, would be bound to cry, "Well, what happened? Did he ever find her?"

"Yes," she would begin again, and she would speak slowly, basking in her conclusion like a cat stretched on a window sill, delighting in the sun. "It was extraordinary. To the amazement of his friends, he did. He was thirty-four, at a New Year's party, just about to leave, as he often did as soon as he'd looked over the crowd, when she arrived. There are a number of stories about what actually happened. Some people insist that he hadn't even seen her face, that she was standing in her hat and coat with her back to him when he turned pale, left a conversation in the middle of a sentence, walked across to her, put both hands on her shoulders, and turned her gently to face him. No one knows what he said to her. But they stood for several moments, he still with his hands on her shoulders, once taking her chin and tipping up her face while he spoke, she a little surprised but making no effort to move. Everyone in the room who knew him knew what was happening, saw a kind of rapture and disbelief come into the face of the dark-haired girl who stood, still in her coat, snow still on her hair and shoulders, long arms hanging helpless at her sides, the room full of people and her husband, a young doctor who stood nearby speaking with the hostess, forgotten. They looked like lovers, oblivious, and his triumph reflected in her face and over the whole glowing room. Later, when she was reclaimed by her trembling husband and whisked away in tears, my friend was surrounded by anxious acquaintances expecting the worst. They were surprised. That his dream wife was married to someone else seemed not to phase him in the least. He celebrated until dawn. That the girl existed and that his passion for her was real appeared to be enough for him. He never tried to see her again, not wanting to upset her life, he said. He lost interest in the Victorian cottage and six months later was married happily to someone else."

Here the woman might stop speaking. After all, she would have to stop sometime. And really wouldn't she only have spoken so long as it seemed worth her while? If she weren't attracted to her listener, if he aroused in her no sympathy or excitement, why bother to go on? And why bother with a man whose very willingness to listen on and on must seem a weakness. Had he no motives or any future? Why, it would be a waste of time, and she would grow bored with herself and her stories and ideas, just the way people don't follow their own silent thoughts too far alone in their heads unless these thoughts have some connection to a driving need or purpose in the world. This might be why, aside from any fear, you and I are often silent when we're together, not knowing whether there is any reason we should speak.

One final thing I think, waiting for you to look at me before you leave, remembering how strange it is that eyes can say so much. They have told me more than words or bodies have. I've never known rage, joy, terror, or death depicted better than by eyes. They are like an ever-changing haiku, a brief, brilliant summation of the whole person and the whole moment. It's things like eyes that make me believe in perfection, because there is no getting away from the truth of them. I think of your eyes when they grow soft and warm, the way your whole expression, normally so closed and stiff, blossoms. I've noticed this, and it's sad the way I often equate a completely open and excited face looking full into mine with sex. Sad because the intimacy that eyes can promise is often more than sex can fulfill.

I wish we were just finishing a lively conversation that left us both refreshed, or that you would ask me at least one question before you leave. But I'm a fearful dreamer. I've read that people deprived of their dreams become psychotic. I've also read that the most enlightened man never dreams, and if he does, he thinks it a bad sign.

Your face is an assault of smiling reservations, an unenlightened but intelligent face like my own; a face best able to express its most enduring conviction when you lie perfectly still in a deep sleep.

Storms and Wars

Before I got my powers everything was different. All that time right up to my eighteenth birthday, it was smooth and peaceful. Always the same. When I saw somebody downtown, they said, "Hi, Billy." They smiled. Nothing was wrong with them. They were all fine. Everybody was, and they never changed.

Back then the weather was so good. The stars came out and I could see the moon over the fields most nights. Mornings, when I opened up my eyes, the sun was there. Sometimes it could get windy. It snowed and it rained good and hard, but there were no bad storms, never a hurricane like the one last year that scared people to death.

Back then nobody was scared. They didn't need to be. Judge Johnson might get mad once in a while. He'd yell at someone, but there was nobody bad in Hinsdale. Nobody rotten that I knew.

There were a few kids that teased me. Jack Wilson teased me a few times. He called me stupid, said I was a retard. But Tom Stone always stuck up for me. One time he got Jack on the ground and sat on him till Jack was crying.

"I'm sorry, Billy," Tom made him say.

I can remember when the Eagles won the championship every year. It never mattered who was playing. Whether it was Buck Fuller, Bobby Freeman, or Jay Curry. The last game of the season Grandpa jumped up, red in the face. "They won it, Billy!" he yelled. "By God, they won it!" Then he took me by both arms and jumped me up and down. The whole gym was up and jumping, and everywhere I looked people were yelling and laughing and smiling, like Grandpa and me.

It used to be my head was light. I couldn't even feel it. I could run up the drive, hop the steps up to the porch, and it was more like I was flying. Now there's always something in my head. There's people there summer and winter. At night I dream of them and in the day they stay inside me. They never leave. There's Grandpa. There's Jeannie, my mother, disappeared since I was two. There's John McClarren, who shot himself after his barn burned down. There's John's wife, Liz, and their girl, Julie, ten years old. She won't talk to anybody since John's dead. There's Carolyn Codman, the only one that calls me Bill instead of Billy. There's her husband, Nick. I don't like him. There's the baby, Lynn. There's Mrs. Boone. She scares me. I keep away from her, and if she ever comes my way, I turn around and run as fast as I can. There's poor Rooney, Mrs. Boone's old dog. There's Tom Stone, my best friend, and Ed, Tom's Dad. There's Mr. Bessie at the pharmacy, Mrs. Tilly, Abe Knight, and all the people I work for.

After that there's the Eagles, there's the weather, and there's more, enough to bust my head wide open. The older I get, the more there is. Some days my head's so heavy, like a water bucket filled up to the brim. I can hardly hold it up, it feels so full. And some days I'm dog tired, too tired even to say a word.

Grandpa says, "What's wrong with you, Billy? You sick or something?"

"No sir," I tell him.

"You don't look like yourself." He puts a hand on my shoulder. "What's bothering you?"

"Nothing," I say. Certain things I can't tell Grandpa just the way Grandpa never wants to talk to me about Jeannie.

"Don't ask me about her, Billy," he always says. "Didn't I tell you not to ask me?"

❧ ❧ ❧

I eat my supper in a circle. I start with carrots, then a bite of potato, then after that that the meat. Then I go on to the carrots. I try to keep my mind on every bite. Grandpa eats with me. The radio is on. In the summer we put on the Red Sox. All winter long we listen to the news. There's storms and wars and killings and car crashes. Grandpa says it gets worse every year.

Last summer I could eat one bite of meat after another. I could finish up my carrots first if I wanted. Now I've got to think about each bite and pay attention every minute. I can't say much to Grandpa or I'll lose track of myself. It's hard, but I can't quit, because there hasn't been a fire *anywhere* I've heard of, not even on the news.

The night the McClarren's barn burned down, Grandpa and me were eating supper. The phone rings. When Grandpa hangs up, he says," It's a shame, Billy. John McClarren's just lost everything. All his stock, equipment, every blessed thing was in that barn. On top of that Tom Mason says he's got no insurance. He's ruined, Billy. That poor man is positively ruined." While Grandpa was still talking, telling me about the fire, I started eating in a circle. I got that red hot burning at the back of my eyes, the same as I always get, my whole throat closed up tight so I could hardly breathe, the way it happens just before I *know*. Then it came to me if I kept on eating in a circle, there wouldn't be fires. As long as I ate like that Jim Bradley could polish up the fire trucks, sweep down the floors, and play cards all night long with nothing else to do, because he'd never have to leave the firehouse. Just Memorial Day, when the trucks would drive in the parade.

"You want more, Billy?" Grandpa says. "There's plenty of meat left. Some carrots, too."

"No thanks," I say.

"Celtics are on tonight. You want to call up Tom, see if he wants to watch the game with us?"

"Sure Grandpa," I smile. Tom's eighteen, the same as me. We do lots of things together. He takes me riding in his truck. We go fishing. Sometimes his girlfriend, Lois, goes with us. Last month they took me to Canobie Park, and we went on all the rides.

"If you're going to call up Tom, you'd better do it now. Otherwise it will be too late," says Grandpa.

"Sure," I say, but I feel more like I could go on up to my room, fall flat out on the bed, and sleep a year.

My room is Jeannie's, the same one she had while she lived here with Grandpa when Grandma was alive. She had the same walls as me, the same floors, and the same windows to look out. There's a board loose in the closet I pulled up one time and found some of her things. There were some little colored stones, a piece of bright red glass, and a white box. Inside it was a piece of silver chain. I put her picture in the box and I keep it there under the board. It's her old school picture Carolyn Codman gave to me last summer. "You mean you've never seen her picture?" Carolyn said. "I've got one in my yearbook." She jumps up, runs inside to get it. After I saw the picture, she said, "I think you ought to have this, Bill." She got some scissors, cut it out, and gave it to me."

My eighteenth birthday was the one time Grandpa talked to me about Jeannie. Grandpa made me a cake. He lights up all the candles, puts it down in front of me. "Now make a wish before you blow them out," he says.

"I wish," I said to Grandpa, "you'd tell me about Jeannie."

Grandpa didn't look too happy. He sighed. "All right," he says. "You're almost grown up. I guess you have a right to know about your mother. But there's one condition. Don't you ever ask me about her again. You promise, Billy?"

"Yessir," I said.

"Blow out the candles first," says Grandpa. I blew them all out with one blow.

⁂

"I wish I could tell you something nice about her," Grandpa said. "But she was no good, Billy. It's sad, but it's the truth. When she was six years old they caught her stealing in Duffy's. Her pockets were full of things." Grandpa shook his head. "She was always coming home with things that weren't hers. We'd ask her where they came from and she'd reel off a good story. I never met a person in my life that lied as much as Jeannie. It was just natural to her to tell a lie." Grandpa sighed. "She was always in trouble. We tried everything to keep her in line, but no punishment, nothing we ever did made the slightest difference. The older she got, the worse she was. The high school suspended her six times. They caught her smoking, cheating, fighting. I can't remember what else. It seemed like every time I came home your grandma was crying over Jeannie, something she'd done. She made herself sick over that girl." Grandpa was quiet. He sat still, looking at the floor. "Jeannie could put up a good front," he went on. "She'd tell us she was sorry and turn on the tears, but there was no truth in her. All her life she was like that, ice in her veins. She cared for no one but herself." Grandpa bit his lip. "I hate to think of her," he said. He looked at me. "She used to sneak out of the house at night and go with one boy or another. There were so many, nobody knows which one it was that fathered you. When she found out she was pregnant, she ran away. Jim Henry happened to be in Randolph a few weeks after she'd gone. He saw her drunk on the street with some man. He tried to get her to come home, but she ran off. We called the police, but they never found her. She just disappeared.

"For three long years there was never a word from her. Your grandma got sick, her health broke down from worry, and she died at the end of that third summer. She was just forty-two years old. Her doctor said it was anemia and heart trouble, but if it wasn't for Jeannie, I know she'd be alive today."

"Four months after your grandma died, Jeannie called home. She never asked about her mother. She was desperate, flat broke down in Florida. She was looking for money. She told me she hadn't eaten for three days. I asked her what happened to the baby. She said you were born three months early, brain damaged. She'd kept you for two years. Don't ask me how or where she kept you all that time. She said you were too much for her, you needed special care, and she'd put you in a state home outside of Randolph, close to Cedar Falls. Of course I thought she must be lying, but I decided to look into it. Well, that was how I found you," Grandpa said. He looked at me. "Jim Henry drove down with me. We found the place, and all I'll say is that it's a blessing, Billy, you were so small that you can't remember it. It was terrible. Half-dressed, dirty kids and grown folks thrown together, all crippled or retarded. You should have heard the noise. A person would be better dead than to live in a place like that. That's what I thought."

"I took to you the minute I first saw you. I wish you could have seen yourself. You were the cutest little tyke, but you could hardly walk. They said it was a problem with your hip. You were born that way, and there was nothing to be done about it. Later on, when I took you to St. Anne's, they told me there was an operation they could do. After it was done, you had a limp, but you could get around just fine, like you do now."

"It took me almost a year to get custody of you. I went down to see you in that hell hole every week till I could take you home. You didn't say much, hardly talked at all, but you were always happy to see me. You should have seen the way your face lit up whenever I came in. There was a woman there, Mrs. Pitcher. She cared a lot for you. When Jeannie left you in that place, you cried for days, she said. No one could comfort you. You kept calling for your mother. You wouldn't eat. You cried until you fell asleep and the moment you woke up, you went right back to crying. Then on the fifth day you stopped, you took some food, and you slept sixteen hours. After that, she said, you never cried again, as if you'd cried enough your first week in that place to last you all your life. It didn't matter if you fell down, if one of the other kids hit you. You wouldn't cry. She'd never seen anything like it, she said. And you know that's how you've always been, Billy. Plenty of times I've wished you'd cry. Like the time you clipped your finger in the door, lost half your nail. It must have hurt like hell, and I told you to cry. But you wouldn't. Do you remember?"

"Yessir," I said.

Grandpa took out his pipe, fills it full and lights it up. He looked at me. "You know, that year I took you home with me was the worst year I ever had," he said. "I'd just lost your Grandma and I'd been laid off my job for the first time in my life. I asked myself how I could care for you when I could hardly take care of myself. But it was the best thing I ever did. Tattersal hired me for better pay than I'd ever made at the mill, and the work suited me better. Mary McCallister had four children home then, and she said she'd be glad to look after you while I was at work. So everything turned out fine.

"I told Jeannie I had you. For a long time she kept calling, always looking for money. She never asked about you. That was the way she was. The first time I took you to Dr. Ryder, he ran some tests on you and asked a lot of questions. Later, he told me it was Jeannie's drinking that affected your brain, which is why your thinking's slow, and probably all that liquor gave you the bad hip, too." Grandpa shook his head. "Maybe I shouldn't be telling you all of this, Billy," he said, "But you've asked me often enough, you might as well get all of it this one time." He took his pipe out of his mouth and stared at me. " I never told you she was dead," he said. "You always liked to think she might come back. So when I got the news, I kept it to myself. One night five years ago, I got a call from the Florida police. They told me they found her lying on a bench in the town park. They said it was drugs that killed her, alcohol and drugs. So that was how it ended, her whole life wasted, and everyone she touched was hurt." Grandpa sighed. "I guess that's all," he said. "I wish it was a nicer story."

He reached across, put his hand down on my arm. "Now eat your cake," he said.

I started eating, but my throat was dry, cake stuck to it, and I couldn't swallow. I felt funny, like the time I got sick in the boat when Tom was going fast across the lake.

"You all right?" Grandpa said.

I looked at him, but I couldn't talk. I felt so queer, I had to put my head down on the table.

"Jesus, Billy," Grandpa said. He came over, put his arm around me. "I never should have told you. I wish to God I'd just kept still," he said.

All the while my head was down, whirling black inside. My eyes filled up, my nose and throat filled up, like I was drowning.

"You're all upset," said Grandpa. He patted my back, and I started heaving and sniffing and shaking. Once I started, I couldn't stop. Grandpa took me to my room, I lay down on my bed and cried so hard, it scared me. Grandpa got a washcloth, washed my face and wiped it with a towel. Still I couldn't stop. He sat by me on my bed the longest time. It seemed like half the night. "It's all right now, Billy. Everything's all right," he kept saying till I fell asleep. But after I cried like that it seemed like nothing was just right, as if the world changed over in one night and when I woke up the next day it was all different.

❧ ❧ ❧

The first power I got was for the hurricane. Grandpa and me brought the chairs in from the porch. We took the garbage cans down cellar, the shovels and the rakes, the two hoses and the garden tools. We took everything we could inside, and nailed the screen door shut. Then we went downtown to board up Mrs. Tilly's shop. She was so nervous. "I know it's going to be a fearful storm," she said. "Look at my hands, how they're swelled up. It's my arthritis. They never hurt this bad before."

Downtown the windows of the shops were boarded up, and everything was locked up tight. People were scared. I never saw them all so scared. I was scared, too.

That night Grandpa put the truck in the garage. "We might as well turn in," he said. "We've done everything we can do." Grandpa went to bed. Pretty soon I heard him snoring, but I couldn't sleep. I kept walking in my room, around and around about a hundred times until I heard the wind start up. It was just a bit of a wind at first, but I could tell the hurricane was coming fast. I could picture all the houses blowing loose, hitting together, and the cars, how they'd be lifted right up off the streets. The trees would rip out of the ground and all of Hinsdale would be flying in the sky, smashed up and wrecked to bits. I kept walking in circles, couldn't make myself sit down, and before I knew it, wind was shaking all my windows, whistling around the house. There was a big crash in the yard, and just when I was scared stiff, I got a vicious hot spell, and the power came to me like that. I went downstairs, put on my coat, stepped right outside. I knew *exactly* what to do. It was raining, wind tossing up the trees, knocking and shaking the garage door like it'd tear it open. Rain hit me in the face, got in my eyes so I could hardly see, but I kept going. Once I got to the highway the wind came up and slammed me on the back like it was going to blow me all the way to town. I started running. Wind was pushing at me, tearing up my hair. The houses by the road were all black, all the people tucked up in their beds. But I ran down the road all by myself, and I wasn't scared a bit.

Downtown were soda bottles, cans and sticks, newspapers and all kinds of things rolling and spinning up Main Street. The air was full of things, all blowing by my head. I saw the courthouse at the end, so big and white, I could see it in the dark. But I kept running, never stopped until I hit the courthouse grass. Then I slowed down, walked right over, I reached out my hand, and the minute I touched the flagpole, the wind died down just like I *knew* it would. I put both arms around the pole and held it tight. The rain stopped and the wind died right away to nothing. All you could hear was dripping everywhere, and pretty soon there were no clouds left in the sky. The stars came out, beautiful and clear, but I stayed on to be damn sure. My clothes were wet, soaked through. Towards morning it got cold, and I was shivering all over, but I didn't mind a bit. I was smiling, and I never felt so good in all my life.

🐝 🐝 🐝

Tuesdays I go to work for Carolyn Codman. It's yard work, mostly, but this summer I painted her garage, and it looks nice. "I never had a better worker than you," Carolyn says. Lots of people say that to me. I like to work. I've always liked to. Sometimes I come home with my sandwich in my pocket. Grandpa pulls it out. "Look at that, Billy. You never ate your lunch. You must be half-starved," he says. But I don't care. I've done odd jobs all over Hinsdale. There are lawns I mowed, windows I washed, trees I trimmed, and gardens and straight hedges I took care of. Wherever I go all over town I can see some work I did.

Tuesdays I walk from our house up to Codman's. Grandpa makes my sandwich. "Say hello to Carolyn for me," he says. "And don't forget to eat."

Our driveway is dirt from the house out to the road. It's full of stones. The big ones look so sharp and mean, I'd like to pick them up and throw them over in the field. But there's so many, I could never get them all. Anyway, I'd be afraid to touch them. The stones are Grandpa's troubles, all the bad things that could happen to him. They're all there on the drive. The big stones are big troubles. Terrible ones, like Grandpa getting killed in a car wreck. The little ones are little things, like Grandpa nicking his face with the razor. I got the power in the spring when Grandpa had a bad flu that wouldn't go away. When I hopped over all the stones and never touched one all the way out to the road, Grandpa started getting well. In a few days he was good as new.

Now I'm careful every time I go out. I get up on my toes and go hopping like a rabbit down the drive. Sometimes Grandpa sees me. "What the hell are you doing, Billy?" He's laughing.

"Nothing," I say. As long as I'm careful of the stones, Grandpa won't have a problem. And he *hasn't*. He's been fine.

When I go out to the highway, I don't worry about a thing unless I have a hot spell. One time there was a red car coming up behind me and I *knew* if I could get to Winham's post box before that car, then Mrs. Tilly wouldn't have arthritis for a week. I took off like a shot and ran so fast, I beat the car. I beat it by a mile, and felt so good I yelled and jumped up in the air.

Richmond Road is Codman's street, and there's a job for me. I've got to watch the lines along the sidewalk, make sure I don't step on one of them. This is for the Eagles. At the start of the season they kept losing. It seemed like they missed half their free throws and most of their three-pointers. Easy ones. "What's the *matter* with them?" Grandpa said. They lost the first three games they played. Then I got the power. It came to me on a Tuesday on my way up to Codman's. I turned hot, started stepping over all the lines. It was that simple, no trouble at all, and that was all it took. Friday night the Eagles beat Manchester High 62-58. After that they had two games home, one game away, they've got a game this Friday home, and they haven't lost one yet.

Sometimes I used to get upset when I was at Carolyn's. I always think of it when I'm heading up the hill. I got upset and wished I could tell Grandpa, but I never did. I was afraid Grandpa might say I couldn't work for Carolyn anymore, and I like to work for her. I've always liked to. I work for her from April to November. Then I put up her storm windows and I quit all my yard jobs for the winter. I don't go back to see her until spring.

Summer days when it's wicked hot, Carolyn calls me up to the front porch to sit with her and Lynn, the baby.

"Why don't you take a break, Bill. Come have some lemonade," she says. She always calls me Bill, never Billy.

"You know, you look just like your mother," she says. "You've got her eyes. And your nose is just like hers exactly. Anyone ever told you that?"

She went to school with Jeannie, and she doesn't mind talking about her. She's told me lots of things. "She was so pretty," Carolyn says. "Much prettier than her picture. The boys were mad about her. My mother told me if she ever saw me with her, I'd be grounded for a year. Jeannie was wild, always getting into scrapes. One time she had an awful fight with Jane Bufithis, right in the school yard, scratched her face so Jane's still got scars. But you know, Bill, everybody's got a good side. I remember one day I forgot my lunch, was sitting in the school cafeteria at noon as hungry as could be, and Jeannie shared her lunch with me. She gave me half of everything," Carolyn said. "Now that was nice, don't you think so?"

"Yes, ma'am," I smiled. I was thinking of Jeannie.

"I know how proud she'd be, the way you've turned out," Carolyn said.

I was watching Mrs. Boone's big yard across the way. Paint's peeling off the house, the yard's a mess. It's full of junk. She never mows her grass, and her front step sags down like it's about to split in two the minute anybody comes to visit. But nobody ever goes to Mrs. Boone's house.

I always hate to see her. She scares me so much. She keeps poor Rooney tied out back. She never lets him loose. When I first saw Rooney, he barked every minute, made a ruckus all day long. He got his rope tied up around a tree so tight, he couldn't budge. Mrs. Boone sticks her head out the window, "Quiet!" she yells, and if he won't stop barking sometimes she comes out, gets a stick and cracks him hard over the head. "Now you shut up!" she says. Rooney's quiet, but just as soon as she's inside, he starts right up again, worse than ever. She keeps him out year round. He's got a little house, but it's not warm. She doesn't care how cold he gets. Winter nights when it's frigid, Rooney carries on and cries till Carolyn can't stand it. She calls Town Hall and the police, but they won't come. They're all afraid of Mrs. Boone.

❧ ❧ ❧

When I work at Codman's, I always bring something for Rooney. I take him some hamburg from the fridge, a bit of frankfurt, or I give him a bite of my lunch. Rooney will eat anything I give him. I do it quick, hide in the bushes and throw the food over the fence. The poor dog looks so bad, his bones stick out, like Mrs. Boone never feeds him.

I always say hello to Rooney. One time Mrs. Boone saw me throw some food to him. She came running out. "Get away from that fence, you hear me?" she yelled. "You bother that dog again, I swear to God I'll set him loose on you." Her face was puffed up, red, and she looked mad enough to kill me. She came charging over to the fence and I took off around the house. I never ran so fast. Carolyn let me in. I was shaking all over, so bad I couldn't stop myself. No one scares me more than Mrs. Boone. She scares me sick. The day she ever touches me, I'll lose all my powers flat and die right on the spot. I *know* because I've seen it in a dream. I always dream of Mrs. Boone, her chasing after me and me running till she gets so close I'm yelling bloody murder. Grandpa hears me, comes to my room, and shakes me. "Wake up, Billy," he says. "How come you're having these bad dreams?"

If Mrs. Boone ever turned Rooney loose on me, Rooney would run right over to me friendly as could be and be so happy to be loose, he'd never hurt anyone, least of all me. When he sees me coming, his tail's wagging, he jumps up to the fence. His mouth spreads open, like he's smiling. All the time I'm working, Rooney watches everything I do. He lies there biting on his rope, just like he wants to get free and come over and be with me. As long as he can see me, he doesn't make a sound. Carolyn looks out sometimes. "It's like a miracle," she says. "It's so peaceful, Bill, when you're here and the dog's quiet." She smiles, real happy, like there's nothing wrong and never was.

❧ ❧ ❧

This spring, everyday I worked at Codman's, I went to knock at the back door. Most times Carolyn was in the kitchen with the baby. When she came out, I looked right at her face to see if it was marked. Sometimes her arms were marked all up and down. Sometimes her neck. One time both eyes were black, puffed up so she could hardly see.

"It was an accident," she said. "Somebody hit my car." But I knew Nick, her husband, did it. Nick came home lots of times around twelve noon. He'd see me working, he'd walk by, and never say hello. The meanness showed right in his face. And he is big, the biggest man I've seen. He went up the front steps, banged the front door shut so hard, it shook the house. He always banged it. Then the birds stopped singing, and everything got so quiet, you couldn't hear a sound the whole time Nick was there. When he came out, he stomped down the steps. I watched him go. He roared up his engine and ripped off in his black car. He drives fast. I've seen him go by lots of times, drive right through town as fast as hell, like he'll hit anything that gets in his way, and he won't care a bit.

I started to feel sick whenever Nick came home. He passed me on the walk, that mean look on his face, and when he went inside, I felt sicker and sicker, like I could lean right over and throw up my whole breakfast on the grass.

One time I heard him yelling. Carolyn was crying, pitiful and scared, and I could hear the baby, Lynn. She's crying, too. "PLEASE!" Carolyn's crying. I'm standing in the yard, don't know what to do. So I took out the power mower, got it running, and I mowed a circle all around the house. I started singing loud enough so Nick could hear me, "I've Been Working on the Railroad", "Row Your Boat", and every song I knew while I was mowing. I went around and around the house. I sang so hard, my head was splitting. Then I felt it come, the burning back of my eyes, my throat tight, like somebody's got me by the neck, and I started sweating bullets, because I *knew* I had the power. While I was still singing, I saw Nick come out the front door fast. He went down the walk, like somebody was chasing him. I wanted to yell after him and laugh right in his face, but I kept mowing and singing till the whole yard was done.

After that I made damn sure the grass was mowed down every week. Mowed right to the ground. I never let it go.

Last Tuesday Carolyn said, "You mind not singing so loud, Bill?" "Lynn's sleeping and it's bound to wake her up."

"I've *got* to sing loud," I told her. She stood there, real surprised, but that was all she said. There are no marks on her. Nick hasn't touched her. He doesn't come home at noon much anymore. I haven't seen him downtown either, which is fine with me. It doesn't matter if I fixed him, I still hate to see Nick Codman.

Grandpa always told me I was special. "You ever notice, Billy, how people warm up to you? When they see you coming, they look so pleased. They pat you on the back or put an arm around you. They're always happy to see you. Now with most people they don't act that way. It's because you're special. Did you know that?"

"Yessir," I said to Grandpa.

Some powers come to me just when I need them. Every week there's more, so by the time I'm fifty maybe there won't be much left to fix.

Wednesdays I work for Liz McClarren. She's got to sell the house and all John's land, but no one wants to buy it. When you turn up their road, you can see the barn burnt down to nothing but a heap. The ground's all black around it. When you get up close, you can still smell the fire. Julie's sitting on the fence, watching for me. I wave to her, say "Hi, Julie," but she doesn't move. When I get there, she hops down, starts after me. All day she follows me around the place, out to the field, when I take out the trash or paint the chicken coop. Wherever I go, she's right behind me, her mouth all squinched up tight. Liz says she doesn't know what to do with her. Daryll is back at school, but Julie won't go, and nobody can make her. She won't talk, hasn't said a word to anybody since John shot himself.

❦ ❦ ❦

Wednesday night I come home late. Grandpa says, "I've got some bad news, Billy. Ed Stone had a heart attack today. They took him to St. Anne's. It's pretty bad. He's having surgery tomorrow. Tom called about an hour ago. He wants to know if you can work with him this Friday. He says he'll need the help."

"Sure, Grandpa," I say. Ed Stone, Tom's dad, owns Newtowne Grille. I work for Ed all winter, washing dishes. Tom works there, too.

"Don't look so scared," says Grandpa. "Ed's not dead yet. Lots of people have heart attacks, get over them, and they go on to live for years. I wouldn't be surprised if Ed pulls through. Now take your coat off and go wash your hands. I've got supper ready."

There's hamburg, French fries, and green beans all set in a circle. I start with French fries and I try to keep my mind on every bite.

"I'm thinking," Grandpa says, "maybe you should go up to Codman's in the morning, put up her storm windows. Tell Carolyn you've got to work with Tom and you won't be back till spring." Grandpa sits down. "I bet Ed will pull through. You know how tough he is. Of course, Tom's worried. You should call him."

"Yessir," I say. Last year Tom finished high school. Now Ed wants him to go away to college, but Tom doesn't want to. He's happy in Hinsdale and he likes it working at the Grille.

Ed gets so mad at Tom, he blows his stack, like he won't stop yelling till Tom leaves town. Ed used to be so nice. When Tom and me were little, he played ball with us. He took us skating lots of times. Ed was a great skater.

"Try to eat your supper," Grandpa says. "Maybe we'll go over to the hospital tomorrow night to see Ed. Would you like that?"

I smile.

"But Billy," Grandpa says, "I want you to get some sleep tonight. I want you to go to bed right after you eat, you hear me? You look so tired. I've never seen you look so tired. Are you sure you feel all right? You don't feel sick?"

I'm not sick," I say, but I don't feel right. On top of that I've lost track of my supper, can't remember if I took a bite of beans or whether it was hamburg, and it scares me. I can see fires starting up all over, bad ones, and no one to blame for it but me. "I can't eat anymore," I say.

Grandpa sighs. "You hardly touched your food."

❧ ❧ ❧

When I get in bed, it's pretty dark out, but I can see some birds come shooting by the window. They come all of a sudden, take me by surprise, and I jump up like they're after me, and let out a yell. There's a dog that barks all night now, down the road. It makes me think of Rooney. Of course poor Rooney's too far away for me to hear him. But Mrs. Boone is right there in my head, waiting to chase me down. She'll come after me the minute I shut my eyes. I *know* it. She wants to get me so bad. She runs and runs, gets close enough that she starts smiling, reaches out her hand. Just one touch, that's all she needs, and BAM, I've lost my powers. I hate to sleep now. I lie there, my eyes wide open in the dark, and pretty soon I see Julie McClarren. It's like she's right there in my room, she looks so real. "Hi,

Julie," I say. Her face is squinched up, watching me, but she doesn't say a word.

❧ ❧ ❧

Next day Grandpa says, "I swear it doesn't seem like November." He's got the back door open wide, it's so warm. I've got a brand new winter jacket Grandpa bought me, but I've never worn it once. Every day's so nice, all I need is my old red sweater.

Grandpa gives me my sandwich. "Say hello to Carolyn for me," he says.

When I stop on the porch it looks like there's a thousand stones, big, mean ones popping up all over the driveway. So many stones, they scare me. But I get on my toes, hop down the drive just fine, and never touch one stone. By the time I get out to the highway I'm so tired, I could lie down by the road and rest right there. But I keep walking, no hot spells at all. Today it seems like the highway is so long, it'll take six hours to get to town.

At Richmond Road I'm careful of the lines on the sidewalk. Grandpa and me are going to watch the Eagles play Dunbarton High this Friday night, and Grandpa's all excited. "Jesus, they've gotten so good, Billy," he says. If they keep on like this, they'll win the championship for sure."

Up the hill old Rooney's barking loud enough that Mrs. Boone is bound to come outside and crack him with a stick, and I hope I don't see her.

I brought some ham for Rooney. He sees me, comes flying over to the fence. I put out my hand and Rooney licks it with his rough, old tongue. I take out two good slices, throw them over to him. Rooney's so hungry, he grabs the ham up in two bites. Then he lies there, biting on his rope. He doesn't make a peep.

I've got to clean the windows first, then slide up all the screens and snap in the storm windows just so. It's hard work, but I don't mind. I like to work.

By afternoon the sky's all dark, like rain, and it starts getting chilly. When I've finished with the windows, I take out the mower and mow the grass down, right up to the house. All the while I'm singing loud. Carolyn comes out behind me, taps me on the shoulder. "Don't bother with that grass, Bill. You can just leave it," she says. "You know, it's *cold* out here. Aren't you cold?"

"No, Ma'am," I say, and I keep mowing. I'm thinking of Carolyn, what happens to her now that I can't mow the grass all winter? I never thought of it before, and it scares me.

When I'm all done, I go to the house to get my pay. "You know, Bill, next time you see me I'll have another baby," Carolyn says, patting her stomach. "It's due the end of March," she says, and I can see how big she is. I never noticed it before. "Now you take care," she says. "Lynn and me, we'll miss you."

I stop by the fence. Rooney's lying in his house, just his head stuck out the door. "Good-by, Rooney," I whisper to him. "I hope it's not too cold for you this winter." Rooney's head is turned up, his mouth wide open, smiling. He watches me go. I turn around to see him, and once I'm on the street, he starts to make a ruckus. I can hear him all the way down Richmond Road, and it makes me feel sad.

It's getting dark, real cold now. And just when I'm wishing I had on my new jacket, it starts snowing. I stop, put back my head, and I can see the whole sky is full of snow, the first snow of the year. It comes down heavy on my face. I've never seen snow come so thick and fast. I watch it hit the ground and pick up on the sidewalk, filling in the lines, so pretty soon, if I don't hurry up, there won't be a way in hell to help the Eagles win this Friday night. There won't be a way to help them all this winter, not if it snows, and I never thought of that before. I never thought of winter and the snow, that's how dumb I am. A dumb, slow-minded, stupid kid.

I start running, jump over all the lines while I can see them. But when I get to the highway, I stop still, watching the snow. It's coming down so fast and thick all over town. Up at Codman's on the grass, over the sidewalks, and all the way out to the house. The snow is falling on our roof, on the garage, over the yard. I can just picture it. It's falling heavy on the driveway, hiding all the stones. So by the time I get out there tonight, I'll step on some big stone and never even know it, some mean bastard of a stone just big enough to give Grandpa a car wreck, hurt him bad, maybe kill him. The more I think of it, the more I don't want to go home. I may be dumb, but not that dumb.

"Stupid Billy," I say to myself. I pull my sandwich out of my pocket, throw it on the ground, and stomp it with my foot. "You dumb, stupid, fool kid, Billy," I say, and I start hitting myself all over, punch my stomach as hard as I can, slap my face, yank on my hair, pull some of it out, just like I did in school. Miss Monroe yelled at me. All the kids ran up, grabbed me by the arms, held me tight so I couldn't move. Tom was with them.

"It doesn't matter, Billy," he said to me. "Now stop it."

Downtown the lights are on in all the shops. "Dumb fool, Billy," I say. I'm upset, breathing hard and sweating. I stop by Oakley's Drug, just looking in the window. Mr. Bessie's in there, back of the counter. Mrs. Tilly's there. Her sister, Belle, is with her. "Stupid Billy," I say to myself. And Mrs. Tilly looks out and sees me. She waves to me and smiles.

Mr. Bessie walks over, opens the door. "What are

you doing out there, Billy? Heaven's sakes, come in. You look cold." He puts his arm around me and pulls me inside. "Just look at you," he says.

Snow's all over me. Mr. Bessie brushes it off my hair and my sweater. "You all right, Billy?" he asks. "Why don't you sit down a minute. I'll get you a nice hot cup of coffee."

But I can't sit down. I'm so hot, sweat's pouring off me under my clothes, down my sides and down my back. I've never sweat so much before, and my heart's beating fast. My head is hurting, too.

"Something wrong with you, Billy?" Mrs. Tilly says. Her sister, Belle, turns around. She's got on a black coat and a blue scarf that's hanging loose around her neck. I keep looking at that scarf. The color is so bright.

"It's awful late. How come your not home with your grandpa?" Mrs. Tilly asks.

"I can't *go* home," I tell her. All the while I'm looking at that bright, blue scarf, my whole throat swelling up so I can hardly talk.

"Well, why not, honey?" Mrs. Tilly asks, real nice.

Sweat's pouring down my arms, my legs, all of me getting hotter and hotter, so hot I can tell that something BIG is happening, like there's sixty powers coming to me all at once and I'm some rickety blast furnace just about to blow. Before I know it, I walk up to Belle. Belle puts up her hand, but I reach right over, yank the scarf off, turn around and run out of the place, all of them yelling, "BILLY"!

I run all the way down Main Street, slip one time and fall in the snow, but I've still got the scarf tight in my hand, and the next time I see Julie McClarren, she'll be smiling and talking all day long, just like she used to. The power came to me like that. A thousand powers came, and I'm still full to bursting with them, my whole self on fire. I *never* was so hot, like I can fix the whole world in one night, and I know exactly what to do.

On Bickford Street I put my thumb out, and a big fish truck stops to pick me up right off.

"It's a miserable night," the man says, "but it's sure pretty."

"Yessir," I say. The snow's coming down so thick, like it'll bury everything in town, but that doesn't bother me at all. I feel more like it's summer out, I'm that hot, and all I have to go is three miles up the pike to St. Anne's.

When we get there, I've got the scarf tied up around me underneath my sweater. I hop out, all excited, like I've got a thousand things to do, and I go right inside, ask the nurse where I can find Ed Stone. She's real friendly, takes me in the elevator. All the while my two hands are heating up till they're both burning hot, like fire.

I see Ed lying on his bed. He's sound asleep, breathing real hard. He looks so bad, all hooked up to machines. I go right up to him and I know just what to do. I lift up his shirt, put both my hands as hot as blazes on Ed's chest, right over his heart, press down real hard, and burn the sickness out. I can feel it melt like a hard knot under my hands, smaller and smaller till it's all gone away. Ed's breathing soft and easy now, without a problem, and when I lift up my hands, I see red marks, just like burns on Ed's skin. I smooth back Ed's hair with my hand, keep smoothing it back, and I put my face down close to Ed's.

"It's all right, Ed," I say to him. "You're fine now." I can see Ed feels so good, his mouth's curved up, he's smiling in his sleep, and he's *cured* just like that.

I'm running down the stairs so fast, I trip three times, but I don't fall. My heart's beating like fury, I'm in such a hurry. Outside, the snow is almost to my knees. It's coming sideways, shiny white, falling down like walls, it is so thick. Like every inch of air is snow.

But I'm burning up. I never felt so big and strong, a thousand things to do, and sixty tons of snow can't stop me. Nothing can stop me now. I'm starting down the pike and Abe Knight pulls up.

"Is that you, Billy? Do you need a ride?"

"I've got to get to Richmond Road," I tell him.

"Well, hop in," he says. "I'll take you. This is some storm, isn't it?"

"Yessir," I say. My whole shirt's soaked right through with sweat, stuck to me under my sweater, like I get a hot spell every minute and sixty million powers coming all at once, if I don't blow up first.

Abe stops just at the top of Richmond Road. The wind's come up. Snow's everywhere. "Jesus," Abe says. "I can't see a thing. Is this where you want to be?"

"Yessir," I say.

"You take care now, Billy," he says. Then he drives off real slow.

I can hear Rooney right off, barking and wailing long and high, just like he's hurt himself, he sounds so bad. It's pitch dark, no lights on the road. Just two lights on at Codman's. Mrs. Boone's house is so black, I can hardly see it. But I know she's in there. Rooney smells me coming, quiets down all of a sudden, and pretty soon I see him switching his tail. He's all excited.

"Hi, Rooney," is all I say. I'm nervous. I know exactly what to do, but I've never done a thing so bad. I'm kicking up the snow right by the fence. I've got to find six good-sized stones. Rooney's watching all the while, biting on his rope like crazy. Pretty soon I've got the stones. I'm walking through the snow, and everything's so quiet, like there's nothing there. When I stop up close to Codman's house, I start pissing in my pants and I can't stop it. I can feel the piss go down my leg like fire. I throw the first stone, and it smashes through the window, wicked loud. I throw off the next one as hard as I can, and I hit another window square in the middle. If I can smash six windows with six stones then Carolyn will be safe for life. That's the power. I throw another stone, and it goes through. The light comes on upstairs. Just behind me, Mrs. Boone's house starts to light up, too, and the whole yard gets bright. Then Mrs. Boone yanks up a window.

"What the *hell's* going on out there?" she yells.

But I just throw a stone. The downstairs lights come on, and the yard's so bright, I'm all lit up. I throw off two more stones, one right after another. They both smash through, and I jump in the air, I feel so good. Then I start running, the yard's bright as day, and I can see six windows with six holes.

Mrs. Boone's outside. "You *better* run, boy!" she yells, and she's after me. I get out to the road, but just then I hear Rooney barking, like he's calling to me, and when I turn around, I see Rooney jump his fence, fly right through the air, and come down running free around the yard. Mrs. Boone sees him, too, and she stops still.

"Rooney!" she shouts at him. But Rooney's leaping, he's tearing all over, like he's so happy, he's gone crazy. It makes me smile to see him. I stand there watching till I laugh out loud.

"Rooney!" Mrs. Boone keeps saying, and she's after that old dog, sliding all around the yard. But Rooney gets away each time, and Mrs. Boone is mad enough to kill him.

"Bastard!" she screams at him. "Wait till I catch you! Just you wait!" she says, and she slips, falls hard in the snow right on her face. Rooney whirls around, starts running towards me, fast as hell. Then I see car lights coming full speed up the hill. Rooney's almost to the road. I'm running toward him.

"Stop Rooney," I'm calling, but Rooney's flying,

jumps right off the curb into my arms, and knocks me down. Then the light comes blasting up, and just before it hits us, I see it's Nick Codman's big, black car.

The next thing I know, I'm flat out in the snow. There are flashing lights and people all around. Rooney's on top of me, like a ton of weight on my chest. I've got my arms around him tight, and he doesn't budge. Mrs. Boone steps up. She's looking down at me, her two eyes shiny, black, and mean. I twist and turn myself, but Rooney's such a weight, I can't get up. Mrs. Boone's just watching all the while, then starts smiling, like she knows she's got me now. Blood's coming up my throat, it's filling up my mouth and running off my chin. Mrs. Boone leans over me, smiling. She puts out her hand, reaches down closer and closer. Then she touches me and she finishes me like that.

There are fires starting up all over town. I can hear Jim Bradley's trucks, all the horns and sirens going. And there are ambulances, rescue trucks keep blazing by, like there's a thousand heart attacks and crashes, people getting hurt so bad. Blood's everywhere. It's pouring out. The snow's all red with blood. They pick me up and I'm so light, I feel like I'm floating up higher and higher, till I'm so high up, I can't hear a thing in the world.

❧❧❧

It's so nice. I lie down in the field, lie in the grass just like a kid with nowhere to go and nothing to do. Sun's coming down so warm and bright all over. I turn my head and I see Rooney lying right beside me. I watch him roll over, rub his back down in the grass, and turn his belly up to get the sun. It makes me smile to see it. I feel so good, I'm all lit up inside.

There's a long road by the field. Far down it Jeannie's coming. She's so far away that I can hardly see her, but I know it's her. I lie there watching, and I feel so peaceful, like I'd never want to move. She gets bigger and bigger, steps off the road. Her hair's loose and she's got on a white dress. I just watch her. She's coming over the grass.

"Billy," she says. She starts running, her arms out to me. I sit up. She's coming so fast. Then I hear Grandpa calling my name.

"Billy. Billy, *please!*" he's calling. Jeannie slows down, stops right in the middle of the field, like she hears Grandpa. Rooney perks his head up, too. "Billy, please!" Grandpa keeps saying. The whole field is turning dark. "Can you hear me, Billy?"

"Where are you, Grandpa?" I ask. I can't see a thing now.

"I'm right here, boy," says Grandpa close by my ear. "Open your eyes." But I feel like I hurt all over. I can taste blood. I'm stiff, and my whole body hurts so bad, I'm scared to move. Grandpa puts an arm under my neck, lifts me up, and my head falls back, so light, all emptied out. All the people, everything is gone and there is nothing there.

"I lost them, Grandpa. I lost all my powers," I say.

Grandpa's whole arm is shaking. "Open your eyes, Billy. "Please," he says, all upset. So I look up.

"Well, thank God," Grandpa says. His old face is looking down at me, all twisted up. "I thought I'd lost you, Billy. I thought I'd lost you for good." Grandpa's crying.

I reach up, touch his face. I put my arms around him tight, and I came back like that.

Sundays

She couldn't remember when he'd started lying down on Sunday afternoons. He hadn't done it when they first were married. At least not regularly Now he seemed to do it every week, each Sunday sometime after four. She'd notice the sudden quiet in the house when he lay down, but then she would forget it, lost in some task. She'd be watering the house plants, sweeping up the hall, straightening her desk or cooking, humming to herself and peaceful in the way she only felt when she was busy. Of all the days she liked Sundays the best. The other days went by so fast, they jumbled all together. But Sunday was long. The hours passed slowly, with dignity, like time out of her childhood. She could catch up on things she'd missed or put off all week long while she was out at work.

She liked to bake on Sundays. She made pies and breads or muffins. All the things he liked. She'd prepare a roast of lamb or beef or chicken with potatoes. The kitchen windows steamed up in the winter and the cooking smells spread through the whole little house until it was so warm and homey that it seemed to cry out for the child they'd lost, the tiny girl who lived only one day, whose perfect little face was still so real to her that when she thought of it her hand would fly up to her mouth and she would sometimes throw the kitchen door wide open to the chill, and let the frigid air pour into the cheerful, steamy room.

It always took her by surprise to find her husband lying down. She'd be carrying up the laundry or headed to the bathroom when she'd pass the open bedroom door and see him on their bed. Sometimes she'd hurry past the door without a word as if the sight of him embarrassed her. She couldn't imagine lying down during the day doing nothing. Just the thought of it made her jumpy. If he'd only sleep, it wouldn't bother her so much. But he never did. He lay there wide awake, and he looked unlike himself. Sometimes not even gazing out the window, but staring up at the empty ceiling in a way that made her think of someone very old. Yet he was only thirty-five, a burly, lively man. He looked out of place, lying so still.

Why shouldn't the poor man rest, she told herself? He worked hard all week long. He was up before her every morning, wide awake the moment that he rose. She'd wake to the sound of him whistling in the shower and have to wrench herself up through a wall of sleep and hurry down to fix his breakfast. She'd have his eggs done over light, his dark rye lightly buttered and his coffee steaming in his cup by the time he appeared with his briefcase in his hand.

"I don't know why you make yourself get up. I could just as easily eat out," he'd said hundreds of times. She didn't have to be at work till ten.

She stood at the window when he left the house. He liked to walk the mile down town to catch the train to work. Even in winter he went off through ice or heavy snow as though the weather couldn't touch him. He had a light, springy walk for someone so large. She'd never seen another man who walked exactly as he did.

❧ ❧ ❧

He didn't watch TV or listen to the radio or read when he lay down on Sundays. His stillness and his silence fascinated her. When they went out to parties, people hurried up to greet him. They gathered all around him. He was such a talker and a storyteller. She was shy in groups. She never laughed or joked or became close to many people at her job the way he did. He was always calling her to see if he could bring somebody home to supper. Yet when they were alone together, he was quiet. She did most of the talking, as if there were no end to all the things she'd like to tell him.

"Tom?" she said one Sunday, stopping at the bedroom door. He turned and looked at her with a little smile. He was never startled, not at all like her.

"What were you thinking about just then?" she asked. "You looked a million miles away." She stayed in the hall, anxious to resume her work.

"Not anything really," he replied.

"You must have been thinking of something," she insisted. Her own mind was never still or empty. It was always focused hard on something: something bothering her or pleasing, something coming up or in the past. It never stopped. Not even at night when she lay down to sleep. Her mind was always ticking.

"Come here," he urged her, smiling like a cat, as if her irritation were amusing to him.

"Not now," she argued, but drawn to him and giving him her hand.

"Just for a minute," he said, pulling her down on the

flowered spread till she rested her cheek on his great chest and felt his chin at the top of her head.

"You fit against me perfectly," he whispered with his arm tight around her.

"I've got a million things to do," she said, all wiry with thoughts and wanting to jump up before the lethargy descended.

"Just lie here a minute," he said in a way that made her give in to the warmth of his shirt, the smell of his cologne, and the silence building in the house till she could hear the birds outside so clearly and see their shapes streak by the window. The sky was violet or pink and she could feel the sweetness of the fading room begin to lull her.

"You're a devil," she sighed, tipping back her face to gaze at him.

"I love you, May," he said, kissing her forehead and her hair. He never wanted to make love on Sunday afternoons. Only to hold her in the stillness for half an hour or more until it seemed to May that a spell came over them, a heavy sense of peace, as if the whole of life had swept away from them in a great wave and they'd become as motionless and changeless as the rocking chair beside the window, the tall white dresser and the row of pictures on the flowered wall that grew more dim and less distinct each minute in the dusky room. She imagined the darkness growing in the house, filling up the unlit rooms downstairs, the empty kitchen growing desolate and grey and disappearing, until she suddenly jumped up from the dark bed and with a beating heart she hurried like a child from room to room, snapping the lights on.

"What are you doing?" Tom's voice trailed after her. "May?" he called. She couldn't answer right away.

Downstairs the darkness seemed immense, so black and thick that it wouldn't lift until she'd turned on every light. The living room, the hall and dining room were all ablaze as she pushed through the swinging door into the kitchen, flipping on the ceiling light, and hurrying across the wide linoleum floor to press the buttons that lit up the stove and counter tops.

Outside, the darkness had become completely solid, sealing itself around the brightly lighted little house. May stood in the middle of the kitchen. She could see herself sharply reflected in the window. A young woman with an urgent, serious face and brown, disheveled hair was leaning towards her, meeting her eyes. The woman in the glass was paler than she was. She looked chilled and ghostly, her folded arms gripped tight against her chest, like someone who had been cast out into the cold, dark air and now stared in with longing at the cheerful, lighted room.

FIFTEEN

It was August first, the hottest day all summer. It was hard to breathe, it was so hot. I was fifteen, mowing the front yard, and I was hurrying to get it done before my Dad got home. My sisters, Lynn and Christie, were on the front step, playing cards, and I could see my mother in her garden down the hill. Fred was with her. It was so hot that when she came up to the house, she turned on the hose and let the kids run through it. Fred kept falling on the ground. His diaper got so wet, she took it off and let him run naked.

"Look out, Tom," she called. She turned the hose on me. The water was like ice, but I stopped mowing, turned around and let it hit me in the face and on the chest till I was cold right through. Mom kicked her shoes off, aimed the hose straight at the sky. The kids all stopped to watch her. She turned her face up and she shut her eyes. The water fell down on her like a shower till her hair turned dark, her dress stuck to her back, and we could see how thin she was. After a while she hosed down her feet, put on her shoes. Then she turned the water on the girls and Fred while they ran all around the yard, screaming so much, I wondered what Dad would say if he drove up and saw them. He might think it was funny, take the hose and spray the kids himself. Or it might make him mad as hell to see Mom dripping wet and the baby running naked in the yard.

Mom was chasing Fred, waving the hose. She always let things go too far. Fred was laughing. His hair was plastered down and he was shining wet all over. He kept falling. I could see his mouth was turning blue. He ran at me, grabbed hold of my leg, and he was screaming bloody murder. I could feel him shaking, his whole body shivering and cold.

"That's enough," I said to my mother. She looked surprised, but she put down the hose and shut it off. She got a towel that was hanging on the line, wrapped Fred in it. She picked him up, and the girls went after her inside.

I kept mowing. The grass was soaked in places and the front walk was all spattered. Dad never liked to wet the grass till after dark, and I hoped it would dry out before he saw it. Grass stuck to my shoes and built up on the wheels. I was worried it would choke the motor, but I kept going. All I wanted was to finish and get up to my room.

❦ ❦ ❦

Every night, when he came in, Dad said, "Where's Tom?" He never asked about the others. He had to know where I was, what I was doing, as if I was up to something.

"Don't you ever let me catch you lying to me," he said to me one time for no reason. Mom stood up for me.

"Why would he lie? He never lies," she said to him. Dad shook his head and walked away, disgusted.

When he was feeling good, he liked to sing. Some nights he piled us all into the truck and took us for a drive. We stopped at Richter's and he bought us ice cream. We tossed the ball with him out in our yard, we'd smile and play with him the way he liked, but I never trusted him.

He hit all of us, but he hit me hardest and the most. I had a dream one time when I was small that he came to my room, sat by me on my bed. "Tommy," he said. "I'm sorry. I don't know why I hurt you. It makes me sick to think of it. He hardly ever called me Tommy. It was always Tom, and in the dream he looked so sad that when I woke up and I saw him eating in the kitchen, I ran to him, hopped onto his lap, and leaned my head against him."

"What's this?" he said, surprised. He was stiff all over, but he didn't put me down.

❧ ❧ ❧

When I was fifteen, he stopped hitting me. I was the only one he didn't touch except for Fred, but he yelled at me all the time, more than he ever had before. Just the sight of me could make him mad. "Son of a bitch if you aren't lazy," was the kind of thing he said if he saw me lying on the couch. I never stood up to him. He was six foot four, two hundred pounds at least. I thought of all the things I'd like to say to him, but I never said them. Nobody talked back to him.

Most of the time I couldn't stand to look at him or be around him, and I felt half-sick when he was in the house, not knowing what would happen. "One of these days I'm going to disappear, "I told my mother. "I just can't take him anymore."

"Don't talk like that," she cried. "If you went off, what would I do? What would I do, Tom, can you imagine? It would kill me!" She got louder and louder, more and more upset, till I told her that I didn't mean it.

Fred was just eighteen months old. All of us loved him, but Dad was a different person when he was with Fred. He changed into a man we didn't even know. If Fred fell down or hurt himself or cried, Dad wasn't mad. He picked the baby up and held him close. He'd talk to him in a soft voice he never used with my sisters, Mom, or me. He'd kiss Fred on both cheeks and on the nose and laugh and smile at him. The girls would stare and stare at Dad when he was holding Fred. Their eyes were serious and wide and they didn't say a word.

When she turned five, my sister, Christie, blew out the candles on her cake and looked straight up at Dad. "Why do you just love Fred?" she asked. "Why don't you love me, too?"

"Now that's the dumbest thing I ever heard," he yelled. "How could you ask me such a stupid question?" You could see the fire in Dad's eyes. He shoved his chair back from the table and stomped out of the room.

❧ ❧ ❧

That day I was still mowing when Dad hopped out of his car. He stopped on his way up the front walk and stood still with his hands on his hips. He was frowning. "Look behind you. Look at what you've left, " he called to me.

I turned around. There was a place I'd missed, but I looked right at him. "I don't see anything," I said.

"What are you, blind?" his voice rose.

I didn't answer him and I started mowing.

"Look at me when I talk to you," he said. "You'll have to go back over everything you missed. Do you hear me?" He was standing by the grass, huge and black in the corner of my eye. "Tom!"

"I hear you," I said, and I threw the mower out of my hands. It fell over on its side, the motor roaring and the wheels spinning.

"What the hell are you doing?" he yelled. "Pick that up this minute."

I didn't move. It was as if I didn't care what happened anymore.

"Son of a bitch," he cried, and he ran at me, both hands out to get me. He grabbed my shirt, but I jerked away from him, turned my back and started running.

Mom came outside. "Tommy!" she called, but I jumped the hedge and started down the street.

"I'll kill that kid," Dad shouted, and I could hear him crashing through the bushes. Mrs. Hughes was in her yard. She looked up, surprised. I felt foolish but kept going. I was thinking he'd stop, but when I turned my head I saw him coming down the middle of the street right after me. The Johnson kids stopped playing. They stared at us, and Mr. Lewis jumped up from the rocker on his porch and stood there watching. We were out in public like a show for the whole town to see, running like two clowns down Creighton Road. I kept thinking that he'd stop, but we went by the grammar school and he was right behind me.

"Bastard!" he yelled. I turned around, and when I saw his face I knew he'd never quit. The more he had to run, the madder he would get, and by the time he caught up with me and grabbed me, I knew he'd beat me down in front of everyone who saw it. I speeded up as fast as I could go, and I headed straight downtown. I thought I'd go to the police station and beg the men to save me. But when I got to Main Street and I saw the sign "Police", I was too scared to stop. I knew he'd put on a good act, he'd win them over in a flash, and they'd give me back to him. So I kept going.

It was close to five o'clock. There were just two men walking ahead of us on the street. They didn't even see us. I turned onto County Road and headed out of town. If I could get far enough, I thought I'd take my chances in the woods.

"Tom!" he yelled. My head was spinning, my throat so dry, I couldn't swallow. I kept running, looked ahead of me and saw Black Mountain rising up above the trees. I knew that I could never go back to our house again. Not after this.

The asphalt stopped and turned to a dirt road. By the time I got there I felt as if I might pass out. There was a sharp pain in my side. I turned around and when he saw my face, he shook his fist at me. There were just the two of us out there, empty fields on both sides of the road, and I wished I'd never left town.

I could see the trees ahead of us. There were ten miles of thick woods that went all the way out to the mountain. Both my legs were shaking, my side was burning up, it hurt so much, and I wanted to be sick. It felt like I was running through molasses, going nowhere. He was gaining on me. I heard him breathing, gasping for air, and when I turned around, I saw how close he was. He'd ripped his collar open and his face was purple. It was twisted like somebody had just rammed a knife into his back. All his teeth were gritted tight, and I could tell he thought he had me. I tripped over a rock, almost fell, and then I got a second wind. I took off like a shot, faster and faster. It seemed like I had never run so fast before, but it was easy. I could feel him falling back. I didn't even have to look. I kept on flying down the road, my eyes so full of sweat that I could hardly see.

The fields were just a blur. I knew he'd never catch me. I could feel him falling away from me, farther and farther away. The heat of the day closed in around me. I was wrapped up tight inside it, and all I knew was the sound of my own feet on the road and myself breathing.

❧ ❧ ❧

"Tom," he called. His voice was just a speck, so far back and so little that I almost missed it. I turned my head and saw him lying like a black heap on the road a quarter mile or so behind me. He was moving, rolling side to side. "Help me!" he cried, and I swung around and stopped. His knees were up and he was rolling in the dirt. "Tommy," he called. I saw his legs go down. Then he lay still.

There were crickets in the grass, millions of them singing together, and it felt like the fields began to move in a big circle all around me. Everything under the sky was moving and turning slowly around and around. I started walking towards him. My shirt was soaked, stuck to my back. I was thinking he might jump up and grab me when I got up close, but he never moved. I stopped about a foot away from him. He was lying on his back, both hands up on his chest. His eyes were rolled up, looking at the sky, his mouth stuck open wide, like he was going to yell.

The sun flashed on a car that was heading out of town. I saw it was Jack Tildon's old, white Chevy, and I started running towards it, waving my arms and yelling.

❧ ❧ ❧

Two days I stayed in bed. The doctor said it was heat stroke. My mother came into my room all the time, wiping my face with a wet cloth, trying to make me drink. She sat on my bed and took my hand, but it was like I wasn't there. When she rubbed my arm, I couldn't feel it.

"Try to sleep," she said. She put the fan on high and left. The shades were down and the room was dark, but I could tell the difference in the house without him in it. The place seemed huge, all emptied out and quiet. The voices echoed coming up the stairs. I lay there listening to them, looking at my room. I thought of how no one would miss him. Never once. They would be glad that he was gone.

Sometimes a breeze blew out the shades, the light came in, and I could look down at the yard and see his truck parked in the drive the same as always. The sun was beating on the hood, and the hot air came into the room. Then the wind died out, the shades sucked back against the screens, and the room was dark. I lay there all day long. The fan went back and forth across my face and every now and then I noticed that my face was wet and I was crying.

I heard them laughing in the kitchen. Fred was screeching and my mother and the girls were laughing. They went on and on until I couldn't stand to hear it.

"Cut it out," I called down to them, but they kept laughing, louder and louder. I jumped off the bed, threw my door open wide so hard, it hit the wall, and I ran over to the stairs.

"STOP IT!" I yelled down, and they all went quiet. I stood there, breathing hard. My legs were weak and I sat down on the stairs, leaned my head against the wall, and shut my eyes.

"Honey?" my mother said. I raised my head and saw her down below. She was holding Fred. "We woke you up. I'm sorry." I just looked at her until a breeze came down the hall and my head cleared. Fred was staring at me, sucking his thumb. He never took his eyes off me.

"Let him come up," I said. My mother put him down,

and he started crawling up the stairs. She came behind him so he wouldn't fall.

"We shouldn't have been carrying on like that, making so much noise." My mother shook her head. She sighed.

"I'll watch him," I said to her.

She stopped a minute. Then she turned around and went downstairs. I lay back on the rug. Fred lay on top of me. I could feel his stomach pumping up and down. I pulled his thumb out, and he smiled. He was all hot and sticky, but he felt good on me. He touched my nose and looked at me with his big eyes.

"Lie down," I said, and he put his head down on my chest. His head was burning hot, the hair all sweaty. I blew air through his hair, and we lay still. The hall was getting dark, and I could hear my mother and the girls putting out the plates and starting supper. Fred's eyes were open. His arms hung down and he lay on me like he'd never want to move. A breeze came down the hall, I rubbed his back, brushed up the wet hair from his neck, and I kept kissing him on the head over and over, like I couldn't stop.

LISTENING AND SPEAKING

I

I am about to take a trip. I will be driving for hours over unfamiliar roads towards a destination I have never seen. My traveling companion is a stranger to me, a blind man named Tim Allen, whose mother hired me to drive him to a city hospital three hours away. Her son was once able to see, but was blinded in a work-related accident. He is also unable to speak. When he leaves me, he will undergo a series of operations that may restore his vision or his speech, but for the duration of this trip, he will be mute and sightless.

As we prepare to start, the man slides onto the front seat beside me. His head is wrapped with bandages, and the expressions on his face are hidden. A metal contraption holds his body upright. It is impossible to tell his age, though I imagine that he might be in his forties. I am sixty-eight years old, a retired music teacher, who taught at the Billings School in Portland for over thirty years. My wife has always struggled with her health and was recently diagnosed with cancer for the second time. Her days are filled with radiation treatments, doctor's appointments and chemotherapy week after week. Often I take odd jobs to make ends meet.

In the parking lot of the large rehabilitation center where we are, Tim's mother offers me a check, which is my payment. She tells me that her son has just received an intravenous feeding and that he wears a bag that will collect all of his bodily wastes. During the trip I will not need to stop the car on his account or move him. She thanks me, shakes my hand through the open window, and then, reaching across my chest, she gently taps her son on his shoulder. "You will be fine," she says, and she doesn't seem to be surprised or disappointed by his granite silence. I notice Tim's hand for the first time, his left hand rising from the seat and fluttering with life above his lap in such a way that strikes me as spasmodic and alarming. Then I realize he is waving. His mother calls good-by as the car glides slowly from the driveway out onto the street, and in an instant she has disappeared from view.

❦ ❦ ❦

I am uncomfortable with Tim at first. I keep my eyes on the road, watching the traffic, following the signal lights and signs. In my life I have met several blind people, but I have not known anybody mute, and never been in the company of a person so doubly afflicted. The full-grown man beside me seems as helpless and as trusting as a child to have put himself so much at my disposal. It occurs to me that I could drive him anywhere; to Florida or the North Pole, and for a while he'd never know the difference. I am not easy with the inequality between us. And yet this silent figure, this mystery person on the seat beside me, has an impact of his own, one that I can't ignore. The power of his presence fills the car, and I find myself aware of sound as I have never been before, of the maelstrom of unceasing noise around us, striking my ears with a thousand messages and clues, as though I, too, have become somebody stripped of sight and speech, whose only channel with the world is hearing.

I speak haltingly to Tim at first, the way I used to stumble on the phone with answering machines when they were first invented, pretending to sound casual and normal, although it was unnerving to send my voice into a void from which could come no comforting human response. But the man beside me isn't a machine, and though he cannot share his feelings or his views, he is made of flesh and blood, a man like me, and this speaks volumes. Sometimes he sleeps. His body slides down slightly in his seat, and for long stretches he remains perfectly still in a world of his own making. At intervals throughout the day, I report to him the time. I tell him how many miles we've covered, and keep him apprised of where we are on the map. The longer I am with him the more I realize how little he perceives, how much he misses, and how destitute his physical impediments have left him. He sits motionless and upright beside me, indicating nothing. The metal cast that stiffly holds his head upright makes it impossible for him to nod or shake his head in disagreement. Yet when I start to speak he often cocks his chin ever so slightly in such a way that makes me sure that he can hear me.

I grow more used to this one-sided manner of exchange. In fact the more I travel with the man, the more careful and considerate of him I am, more than I have ever been in the battleground of ordinary conversation. I do not want to tire him, to confuse him, or to overwhelm him. I pick and choose the moments when I tell him things. Sometimes words fail me, I digress, and all the proper metaphors elude me. Sometimes Tim's head drops forward and he drifts off to the escape of sleep while I am speaking. Other times by some sheer accident of tone and choice of language, I give an excellent description, one that seems to catch the very essence of a person or a scene I am discussing. I feel a thrill of triumph when this happens, as though I had forgotten the purpose of all language and its undying longing for communion.

Time passes, sometimes slowly, sometimes quickly. When I notice it, the road ahead appears to rush right towards me until it disappears at a fierce speed beneath the car. I watch the sun as it sinks lower in the sky, and the view begins to soften as the light becomes more gentle. Each time I am aware of my fatigue, I drink from the thermos of coffee I've kept filled and ready on the dashboard. The further we go the more my right leg aches from this long stint of driving, my head feels oddly light, and my neck and shoulders have grown stiff. The small sandwich I ate at noon was not enough to energize me for so many miles, and my stomach seems to be completely empty.

The road has widened to four lanes and suddenly is crowded with more traffic than I've seen all day. Enormous trucks speed down the hills, passing us with a roar, and rushing cars crisscross the lanes before me and behind me. I find myself gripping the wheel, staring at the scene ahead and in my mirrors with such full attention that for a time I utterly forget the passenger beside me. The sun is now approaching the horizon and turning red, throwing a pink light across the sky and recoloring all the objects on the ground in this kaleido-scopic world where everything appears to be constantly changing. In the distance I begin to see the skyline of a city taking shape. "We're almost there," I say. "About twenty-five more minutes if we're lucky." I think with relief of delivering my companion to the hospital and imagine how much easier the return trip will be. I'll be able to play the radio if I want to, stop to eat for as long as I like whenever I wish. I'll be able to use my phone, call my wife, talk to myself, as I sometimes do, or to sing at the top of my lungs if the impulse hits me.

When we leave the busy highway my concentration goes entirely to the page of neat instructions I have taken from my pocket that will lead us through the final blocks up to The Berwick Hospital. I sink into this map of words where every signpost is a victory when it appears upon the road before us, and soon I see the tall, brick building. The emergency entrance is to the left, as I was told it would be. There is a lighted sign above a wide, revolving door.

"We're here," I say as I pull into the parking lot and stop. "I'm going to go inside and tell them. I'll be right back."

Two orderlies return with me, one pushing a wheel-chair. I look closely at the lone man waiting motionless on the seat, and open the door beside him. "There are some people with me who will help you get into a chair and take you to your room," I explain, stepping aside so that the orderlies can move him.

"I'm going to leave you now," I say at last, looking down at the bandaged face in the chair before me. Tim's right hand appears and rises in the air. It stretches to-wards me and I grasp it. His handshake is far stronger than I had expected, gripping and holding me with surprising force. Is it warmth or fear or gratitude he is expressing? I do not know.

"They've been expecting us. I'm sure everything will be fine," I say, mimicking his mother's shoulder tap as well as her words.

❧ ❧ ❧

I slam the door shut on his side, circle the car and climb into my seat, watching as Tim is pushed across the parking lot. It is nearly dark outside. The air looks almost gray, and my passenger appears to grow smaller and smaller in the chair as he approaches the revolving door until he disappears inside the brightly lighted building. I can feel his presence in the car, my mind still overcome by the disturbing power of his handshake, which has left a throb of feeling in my body that I can't put into words.

II

My home is in the city. This Sunday morning I've arrived at church as I do every week unless I'm ill or traveling at a distance. I've come early, as is my habit. My husband used to be with me, but I have been a widow for three years.

I've taken off my coat, smoothed my skirt over my knees, and am seated in my regular pew, watching the people slowly file into the building and down the many aisles of this enormous room. Soon every row of seats is taken, and when I raise my eyes, I see a similar parade of men and women pouring through the doors upstairs and filling all the benches in the balconies.

At last, there is no empty seating left in the entire church. Latecomers are forced to stand in a great arc along the walls, upstairs and down, wherever there is space to stand. Then the large back doors are closed against the morning chill, and within the church the echo seems to have gone out of the room, as though the air on every side and from the floor up to the high-vaulted ceiling has gathered substance and been weighted down and thickened by this sea of bodies.

The organist finishes the prelude, and the people rise to sing the opening hymn. I stand, as well, adding my voice to the swell of others that follow the same verses, words and lilting melody, as though there were nothing special or significant about the synchronicity of sound and movement this massive group will make an effort to achieve as they kneel, sit, stand, listen, speak, and sing together - in an attempt at unison which will last as long as they remain together in this room.

The cross and its procession move up the center aisle that leads to the altar, and my eyes rise from the hymnal to glimpse the minister of this church as he walks slowly past my pew, a huge figure of a man who towers over most of his parishioners. This is the preacher all have come to hear, whose reputation as a speaker is known not only in this city, but throughout the country and abroad, as well. Many Sundays as I watch him pass, I feel an up-rush of emotion. It is a pleasure to look at any man with so much admiration, with gratitude even for his existence in the world, and an excitement to be in his presence.

I gaze at the people close around me. Louise McCabe has sat in front of me for years, accompanied by her mother and two sisters. Louise, the eldest of the three unmarried daughters, is a forceful, loud-voiced woman. At church events I've heard her words ring all the way across a crowded dining hall. She has a harsh, opinionated tone that hammers other people into silence. Her frowning face reflects the urgency or darkness of her views. When I kneel down in church to pray,

I often put both hands over my ears against the sound of her insistent voice.

The Dodges sit in the left-hand pew beside me. Roger Dodge and his wife Lydia. They are immaculately dressed, a quiet, upright-looking pair, who usually appear to be inscrutable and stiff, their faces swept entirely clean of any mood or hint of what their private thoughts might be.

And yet, one never knows what to expect of people. There have been several Sundays in the past when something made me glance over at Louise McCabe during the sermon. In fact, I stared at her until I almost lost track of the minister. To my surprise the woman's upraised face looked almost child-like. Her eyes were wide and they appeared untroubled, her whole expression peaceful in a way that I had never seen it, as though it was the greatest pleasure to her to be still. And at least two times in the last five years Roger Dodge has turned unexpectedly and smiled right at me for an instant, with a fondness that amazed and touched me, as much as if I'd always cared for this odd man with whom I've rarely spoken. How can a person make sense of such things?

Each week the effect is the same when the minister steps into the pulpit. He stands before the room and says a prayer before he starts the sermon. And at that moment with the window light illuminating his lowered face, an immeasurable quiet starts to build within the room. All coughing stops, nobody clears their throat or sneezes, and soon there seems to be no movement in the church, as if the speaker stands before a hall of statues. Perhaps this is because for all of his enormous size, the preacher's voice does not boom in the least. In fact the people often have to strain to hear his words. If this weren't problem enough, he speaks at a quick rate that only speeds up with each new sentence that arrives. At last, there is a moment when the whole church seems to hold its breath at once, as though the people were all starved to hear and carry off the single nugget of a teaching that he gives to them most Sundays; some view so strange and new, it's like a sight they've never seen before in all their lives, and yet they realize at once that what he's shown them is completely true.

Each time the minister enters the pulpit, I want to put a stop to all the little thoughts that sweep so aimlessly and freely through my head in never-ending, forceful currents that vie and grab so furiously for my attention. Before the sermon starts, I try to make my mind as bare and empty as a prop less stage. I want to give this speaker total access to me, as though each word he utters is a brush stroke I must notice if I am to share his final vision. I ask myself why is it that sometimes my deepest longings appear to be much stranger than I knew and not at all what I supposed they'd be? Now that I've begun to recognize my ignorance, just the shadow of its hovering enormity, why is it that, instead of feeling bleak despair or burning shame, I am uplifted and excited, my mouth dropped slightly open and my breath half-held some Sundays while I listen, as though nothing in the world is more important than this small attempt at learning?

THE SAILOR

A slender, grey-haired man sat fully clothed on the sandy beach, staring at the ocean scene before him. He was in his seventies and had made a long, successful living as a portrait artist. He'd painted college presidents, bishops, governors, judges, corporate giants, their spouses and their children. His work hung all across the country in offices and chapels, along austere, dark hallways, in formal dining rooms, and decorating the walls of private houses he had never seen. Tomorrow he would start a painting of his wife. This had been married fifty years, and this would be his third portrait of her. He hoped to finish it while they were here in Maine for two weeks of vacation.

The painter gazed at the sea. Shining water rode up on the shore under the morning sun and stretched away mile after mile to the horizon. There was the smell of salt in the air, and up above, a long procession of thin clouds glided slowly as a group across a pale, blue sky. The long beach was empty, and for a while the painter was aware of nothing but the sound of sea gulls, the incoming surf, and a whipping breeze that swept across his face until he closed his eyes, tipped back his head and felt the wind blow at his arms and neck and through his hair. It was the sort of day, he thought, when the whole outdoors felt vastly spacious and a man could imagine leaping up and dancing like a child at all the freedom that had opened up around him.

A small parade of people began arriving at the beach with armloads of towels, coolers filled with food and drink, beach chairs, and large umbrellas. At first they settled at a distance, but soon a dark-haired, burly man with a crew cut approached, dropped his belongings close by, and spread a towel on the sand.

"Beautiful day," the painter said to him.

"It is," the man replied, nodding his head. He was wearing bathing trunks, and as he removed his shirt and then his shoes and socks, he revealed a body that appeared (with the exception of his neck and face) to be entirely covered with tattoos. Glancing over at the painter, he spoke almost shyly. "I'm a navy man," he said, as though he needed to explain himself. "I've got a tattoo for every port I've been to and every woman I've loved."

"Looks like an interesting life," the painter said. He smiled.

"Yes," the sailor answered. He sat down on the towel, breathing hard, as though his motions were an effort for him. "I always loved adventure. I've been all over the world and seen it all. Maybe I've seen too much."

"What do you mean?" the painter asked, surprised.

"There's no excitement to it anymore," the sailor said. "Last year I took a train trip, the first time I've taken a train in twenty years. I went places I'd never gone before. I planned it that way. But looking out the window of the train all day, there wasn't a thing we passed that didn't make me think of somewhere else I'd been. It was the same with the conductor, who kept taking tickets and calling out the stops. He was the spitting image of an old buddy of mine, a guy I always liked, who joined the navy the same week I did. I remember the people sitting on that train around me. Nobody stood out, not even a retarded kid who sometimes jumped out of his seat and ran up and down the aisle. I felt at home with everything in sight. As the sun went down, I thought of other nights I'd spent one after another. So this is the beginning of old age, I said to myself. The older I get, the more I'll be like a prisoner locked up in the past. Nothing will ever again be new." He turned toward the painter. "Even this talk we're having is old," he laughed, shaking his head. "I've said these things before. Everything has been said. Do you know that?"

"Not at all," said the painter, sounding shocked. "Your view sounds odd to me. In fact I can't imagine it. Each time I look at things, I see them differently. Nothing ever stays the same. Nothing." He spoke emphatically. "Anyone who paints would tell you that. Take my face," he said, rubbing his chin. I've probably looked at it as often as I've looked at anything in my life. Everyday I see it, and nothing is more familiar or more mysterious to me. I cannot memorize my face. It's always changing."

The sailor shook his head uncomprehendingly and stared at the painter with a frown, as though he'd listened to a moron. He swung around till he lay flat on his stomach with his legs out straight behind him. Then lowering his head, he let his cheek rest on the towel. Closing his eyes, he sighed with something like relief. He realized he was tired. He did not want to think, and yet the painter's words played in his mind like a stubborn song. No matter how he tried, he could not make it stop. "It's true," he thought to himself at last. "Even now this minute, when I think about my face, the picture that I get is fuzzy. I don't know how I really look." He was about to speak, but when he raised his head, there was no one beside him. The painter had disappeared.

That evening the sailor left his motel room and walked to a nearby restaurant. It was early, not quite five-thirty. There were couples eating at several of the tables, but he chose to sit at the long, empty bar, where he ordered a scotch on the rocks. Yesterday, on board his ship, he'd suffered chest pains and shortness of breath, the same symptoms his father had complained of years ago. Although the sailor argued that the pain was mild and brief, and might be nothing more than indigestion, right away arrangements had been made for him to go on shore leave. He was to check into York hospital tomorrow morning for two days of tests.

The sailor was thinking that he'd told no one at home about the hospital, and that there was no family left to tell. He'd married once at twenty-two and was divorced after three years. There'd been no children. He hadn't seen Bernice or spoken to her since she'd shown up at his father's funeral. People in his family died young. Even his only brother, Ted, was gone. Heart problems, diabetes, or cancer had taken everyone but him.

The restaurant was filling up, and people started sitting at the bar. Before he knew it, the sailor had downed four drinks, double the amount he usually drank when he went out these days. It wasn't smart to drink so much tonight, he told himself. But when the waitress stood before him, he ordered yet another scotch.

Before his drink arrived, the sailor stood and slowly wound his way across a room of busy tables towards the restrooms. His balance wasn't good, and someone grasped his arm. "Hello there," a voice said, and when the sailor stopped, he saw a man and woman looking up at him from their table. "We spoke at the beach today," the man said pleasantly. "I'm Walter Kellog, and this is my wife, Jean. We never got around to introducing ourselves when we were talking."

"No," the sailor said. "Now I remember you. I'm Frank Benton." He shook the painter's hand. " I was surprised the way you disappeared on me."

"You fell asleep, and I didn't want to wake you," the painter said.

"Well," it's nice to see you, and to meet your wife," the sailor said, smiling at the blond woman in the brightly colored dress. He was afraid he looked and sounded tipsy. "Enjoy your dinner."

"You, too," the painter said.

Once he'd entered the men's room and relieved himself, Frank Benton caught sight of himself in the mirror. There was nothing unexpected about his face. It looked the same as it always did when he saw himself in mirrors, and if it hadn't looked that way, he thought, it would have scared the daylights out of him. He stared at this mirror face, which he only saw when he was alone without another person present. It was expressionless, and it stayed that way while he washed his hands, revealing no emotion, as though the sameness of this empty face had no more meaning than the trash can on the floor behind him or the light that never flickered on the ceiling. No one else was in the room, and he forced himself to smile at his reflection, noticing how stiff and fake a smile it was. Then, for a moment, he leaned towards the mirror, his hands resting on the sink, while he made faces at himself. His first attempts were timid: he looked mildly strange, then sad and clownish. Soon he bared his teeth and glared with eyes that had grown mean and vicious. He shook his head from side to side as he stuck out his long, red tongue as far as it would go. At last he let his hands fall to his sides.

The sailor stood still, his face now serious and calm, as he looked at himself appraisingly. He was wearing a summer shirt. His tattoos stood out boldly on his arms until they disappeared beneath his sleeves. Part of a pink rose in memory of his mother bloomed on his upper chest from which green tendrils grew in loops out to his hidden shoulders. His tanned, undecorated neck was like an empty stem, reminding him of nothing. Yet on his face the large, sharp nose that took up space was like his father's nose, almost exactly. His coloring and hair came from his mother, but he could see no sign of Ted upon his face, the brother he'd been close to. Ted had been tall and thin. His ears stuck out. Often the family called him Red because of his hair. And now he was dead, almost two years. The sailor's bloodshot eyes stared back from the mirror at him with such ferocity, he couldn't bear to look at them, and turned away. In an instant he had left the room.

As he made his way back to the bar, he avoided Walter Kellog's table. He could see the glass of scotch he'd ordered waiting for him. The bar area was crowded now and his was the only vacant stool. Once he was settled, he ordered a large cheeseburger to go and sipped his drink while he paid the bill and waited for his food. There were men hunched forward on either side of him and the sound of talk and laughter just behind him, where people mingled, waiting to be seated. Ordinarily, he'd have struck up a conversation with someone and eaten at the bar, but tonight he spoke to no one and wanted to leave the restaurant as quickly as he could. The moment his food arrived, he tipped the barman and rose from his seat. The roar of lively voices sounded festive all around him, and he hurried to the nearest exit.

Outside, the summer evening was bright. It was still early with another hour at least before the light would fade. Frank sat down on an empty bench outside the restaurant and leaned against the building. There were few people in sight, and the breezy quiet of the street was a relief. The air was turning cool under a sky empty of clouds. He unwrapped his food and ate hungrily, like someone starved. His mind grew fixed on every bite he took, focused on the flavor of the meat, the cheese, the juicy, sliced tomato and the mayonnaise all warm within the lightly seeded bun, until it seemed his mouth had turned into a small, forgotten chamber that was riotous with pleasure.

When he'd finished eating, he tossed the paper remnants of his meal into the trash bin beside him. Still high from the scotch, he felt like a ghostly version of himself upon the bench. He did not know this town or what he'd do with the empty time before he returned to the motel. He didn't want to go to sleep. Tomorrow loomed before him like an unwelcome country he was fast approaching. Sleep would only speed up his arrival. He put the hospital out of his mind and would not think of it.

For a while he sat entirely sated by the food and wished for nothing, but before long one of his legs began to jiggle up and down impatiently until it came to him that what he badly wanted was a cup of coffee. He stood up instantly and began to walk. He almost smiled, as though it were a blessing to be propelled along the street by yet another strong desire.

At dusk Frank Benton sat in a chair outside of his motel. A row of cars stood parked before the building, but no one was in sight. He missed his friends. Now that he'd left the ship, he felt entirely alone. He mattered to nobody in this town and he cared for no one but himself. A paper coffee cup stood empty by his feet. The light had grown so dim that he could barely see the well-known tattoos on his arms. In fact, his skin looked almost clear, and suddenly, for no reason that he knew, he wished to God there were no decorations on him. His head was throbbing from the scotch, as he leaned forward, holding his downcast face in his hands and shutting his eyes, like somebody embracing darkness. Why wasn't he ever satisfied with anything, his wife used to ask him? Why was he never happy, always wanting more? It ruined everything they did, she cried. He could hear her voice, exactly how it sounded. He used to fend her off, furious and sometimes swearing, shouting her down and drowning out her words. It was terrible how clearly he could hear her now.

Depression

For two weeks the weather is the same. Every day is cold and grey. His mind is equally cloudy. He finds himself becoming obsessive about the sun, longing for it as though it were a vital piece of mail. In recent years his depressions have loomed larger and lasted so much longer, they can't be ascribed to "moodiness" anymore. Not such extended states of lethargy and gloom that arrive for no apparent reason, having the impact of a disease, and appearing to be less an emotional state than a rational attitude.

At twenty-two his past has assumed a certain bulk. When he is depressed, all of his experience measures up to a weight that is surprising, even shockingly heavy. And the burden is offensive. Life was not meant to be suffered like this, he hopes, although the streets are filled with adult testaments to affliction, sometimes in overwhelming numbers. And it may be that they represent reality, all of these grim-faced people with averted eyes: the ultimate truth that each man learns to his own dismay.

He stands on his fire escape, nauseated and pale. None of the people, the movies, or the dinners out has affected his blackness in the least. For three nights he hasn't slept, and he leans out over the parapet toward the instant relief of the pavement below. He rocks back and forth to the thrill of his choice until two stories above, a window opens. A blast of music fills the whole back court, and Mahler pours down over him while he turns up his face to receive the familiar rain of notes. Through all of his melancholy doors the grandeur of the music enters, as though he were the perfect structure and the only vessel for the notes which re-enforce and fill up every inch of him with sounds so passionate and sad that he stands with his head bowed down, his hands hung at his sides, as though his presence had been met with a burst of wild applause.

IN DANVILLE

"Annie, when you think about it, is there anyone you ever hated?" Len's voice sounded strange.

"Why would you ask me something like that?" his wife exclaimed. It was a Saturday, and they were driving to the grocery store.

"You haven't answered my question," he insisted, bent forward in his seat behind the wheel.

Annie sighed, staring at him. Last week he had turned fifty. He was a tall, thin man and his face looked pale in the morning light, as though he hadn't slept well or might be coming down with the cold that everybody had. "I know I've disliked some people in my life," she said, "but I can't think of anyone I've hated."

"I wish I could say that." Len's tone was grim. "I don't have faith in people anymore. Think of all the crime we hear about, and a whole new batch of killers every week."

"You watch the news too much," his wife said. "It's a beautiful day. Why are you talking like this?"

"I don't know." Len scratched his head. Last night he'd dreamed about his father, that frightened, weakling of a man who'd disappeared one day without a word and left his family for good. Most often Len was able not to think of him, and yet last night he'd been invaded for the second time this month; forced to see his father's face up close, like an assault, until he woke up stiff with pain and bleakness in the dark.

"Don't say anything for a minute." Annie sniffed. "I need to concentrate." She pulled her grocery list from her coat pocket. It was as if they had run out of everything, she thought. There was no ketchup or mayonnaise in the house. "Good grief, I just remembered we don't have any eggs," she said, amazed, grabbing a pen from her purse and adding to her list.

Her husband hesitated. "If you look back," he said in the same odd voice, as though he hadn't heard her, "what's the thing that makes you most ashamed?"

"Lenny!" his wife cried. "Are you a priest? You make me feel like someone going to confession. Why are you asking me these questions? I was feeling good until I got into this car."

"I'm sorry, Babe," he said.

Annie was staring at the grocery list, shaking her head as she wrote down orange juice and jam in tiny letters at the bottom of the page. This afternoon she'd need to vacuum the downstairs. The living room was foremost in her mind. Also, the hamper in the bathroom, which was overflowing with their clothes. They'd have to start a wash as soon as they got home. Glancing out the window, she was grateful for the quiet in the car. There was just the blowing of the heater, which she'd turned up high against the January cold. The car was eight years old, and it always took a while before the heat came on. Now they were bathed in pleasant warmth as they drove slowly on the slippery road. The ice was melting on the salt-strewn pavement, and she could see all of the yards and houses heavy with snow from the storm two days ago.

She and Len had come and gone over this stretch of highway thousands of times, but she was never tired of the sameness. Often she told people how much she enjoyed this little town, where everything in sight was so familiar. It was like staring at something you loved again and again, appreciating it from every angle. She was grateful that her husband wasn't looking forward to a million trips when they retired, the way some people did. He was a math teacher at the grammar school and she had been a nurse at Billings Hospital for fifteen years. The older she got, the less she wanted to travel. If Len had thought about it, he'd never have asked what made her most ashamed. He knew all about her fear of planes and flying. She'd been unable to go to Florida with him for his cousin's funeral. She'd also missed her sister's wedding, her nephew's graduation, not to mention other family gatherings that were far away. Over the years her phobia had gotten worse, and she was mortified to be so crippled by a fear.

❧ ❧ ❧

Ahead of them, the store was coming into view. They always bought their food at Conley's Market. They knew just how the products were arranged in every aisle, which made the shopping easy, and they were fond of many of the employees. There was the meat man, Jim; Jean in the cheese shop; Mary-Jane, who oversaw the plants and flowers; Ames and Phil, who stocked the salad bar and produce; Terry Bolton, who was the manager, and all the check-out people. Whenever they were at Conley's someone always asked about their daughter, Julie, who was a freshman in college thirty miles away.

Len spoke. "We're almost there. I hope your list is done." The store was to their left. Turning into the lot, he found a wide, convenient spot to park, close to the main entrance.

Annie reached across and tapped his shoulder. "Honey, you look so tired," she said. "Why don't you sit out here a while and take it easy. Put the radio on and rest for twenty minutes. Then you can come find me."

Len turned towards her, meeting her eyes. "Maybe I will," he said. "I've got a headache. I'll catch up with you." He watched his wife as her red hat and coat passed out of sight. She had a lively, eager walk and liked to wear bright colors. Enthusiasm was the word he thought of to describe her. She had many friends, and was the last person he could think of who could hate anyone. It was stupid to have asked her such an ugly question for no reason.

❀ ❀ ❀

Unlike Annie, who was excited when she talked about their daughter's life away at school, he was anxious about Julie. Often he thought about their only child, wondering where she was right then that minute in a way he never had while she lived with them.

Letting his head fall back against the seat, Len could feel a beating ache in both his temples. If Annie knew just how much anger at the world had built up in him, she'd be horrified. There was nothing hidden about her. All of her feelings showed so clearly in her face. Her voice also gave her away. It was as if she were a person you could know completely.

And yet, he thought, she still was able to surprise him. Her hand, reaching across to pat his shoulder, just as she'd done moments before, had all the power of a wand that touched the dark, disturbing thoughts inside his head and made them disappear.

Len stared across the parking lot, watching the melting snow as it dripped or slid or fell in quick cascades off trucks and cars. It was close to noon and the view around him was so bright that it was almost blinding. He closed his eyes and thought of Julie. Only half an hour away, and yet she might as well be on another planet. Right now his daughter could be in a classroom taking notes or seated in the dining hall at a table by herself, eating her lunch. There was no knowing what she might be doing. She was a quiet, shy girl, and it would take her longer than some people to make friends.

As he thought of this, Len roused himself. He climbed out of the stuffy car, closed the door behind him, and started walking through the windy cold, which seemed to clear his head as it lashed at his bare face and neck until he put both hands in his coat pockets. The humped-up slush across the ground was just as he expected it to be, like something he had memorized from winter after winter until it was as unsurprising as the feeling of a sandy beach under his toes in summer or a grassy lawn, whose look or touch were as familiar to him as the feel of his own hair or the feet inside his shoes, now climbing the two steps to Conley's Market where the entrance doors slid open by themselves, the same as always.

RUIN

I

In all of his life Bob Long had never known brutality. Born in the 1940's, he'd been beloved by both his mother and his father, who saw him as another proof of life's great joys. While he was small they were unendingly protective when it came to anything that might upset or harm him. If they heard unpleasant news, they kept it to themselves and never spoke of it before him. The bedtime stories that they chose to share with their young son were always upbeat or intriguing with an ending that was never sad. The radio in the living room, when it was on, was tuned to music, and later on, when the family owned a television set, the boy was not allowed to watch disturbing programs.

Although Bob's father once had been a soldier in the war with Germany, he never spoke of those two years abroad, as though they hadn't happened, and in the face of hardship always pushed himself ahead without self-pity or complaint. He shoveled out the house and car after a winter blizzard and worked long hours at Severs Hospital as a surgeon, as though he knew that life was never meant to be without its times of strain and periods of struggle, and yet there was no stopping him from taking up each challenge.

Bob's parents were well-suited to each other. They were both social people who looked forward to upcoming parties, games of bridge, croquet or tennis in the summer and vacation travel. For them most weeks appeared to promise a fresh gathering of people, an interesting event, or an adventure. They invited friends to dinner, knowing that these guests would match them in an evening set aside for nothing but enjoyment. Bob's mother was a gourmet cook and the Longs were well-known for their parties. Their house was brightly decorated, immaculate, and lovely down to the last lampshade, photograph, or paintings on the walls. The hosts and guests were fashionable people dressed in handsome clothing and exuding scents of after shave or fresh perfume. The dinner atmosphere was candle-lit and warm, and the food Bob's mother had prepared was elegantly presented and delicious from the first course to the last. Around the table there would be no serious disagreements or any anger. It was meant to be an evening of pure pleasure.

While Bob was young he often fell asleep to the sound of laughter rising from his parent's dining room below. Throughout his early years at school, he was a friendly, cheerful child, who always made good friends, and in this way was similar to his mother and his father. It was only when he reached his early teens that he began to register the enormity of crimes, injustices, and catastrophes that regularly filled the world. Yet as he learned the history of human cruelty and suffering there was a way in which these ghastly facts remained like nightmare dreams that were beyond his understanding.

II

"I feel sorry for his hat, "Bob used to joke when he disliked someone, as though he pitied any piece of clothing forced to be so closely pressed against that person's body. Yet now, this year, when he was thirty-five years old, his own pants were a painful sight. Day after day Bob wore them in the heat of summer. If he fell down on his bed at night, although he couldn't sleep, he kept them on. When morning came, he didn't change them. Each hour these khaki pants became more wrinkled, marked and spattered. They'd never known such treatment. In the past they'd just been one of many sets of trousers. At most he'd wear them for a day or two before they'd be dry-cleaned or tossed into the washer and the drier. The seat of these pants was now so worn that when Bob bent down to retrieve a pencil from the floor one day, the seam across his buttocks ripped wide open. Would this damage to his clothing be enough to bring about a change? Nothing was certain anymore.

Bob's white shirt was badly spotted with blue ink. There was a whorl of ketchup on his chest, cooking oil lining the cuff of his left sleeve, and coffee stains across his midriff from a spill. His checkered undershorts were caught up in the crack between his buttocks. His socks, so long held captive in a broiling pair of shoes, were stretched and drenched with sweat.

Although he'd dealt with disappointments, broken bones, bad sprains and a thousand accidental cuts or burns or bruises, no pain in Bob's whole life had ever hinted at the agony that now had lodged itself within him. It was anguish so enormous that he felt extinguished and unhinged. He was alone in his house, and by the grace of God no one could see him. For once it didn't matter how he looked or what he said. He'd locked his doors and lowered many of the window shades until he felt like someone who had been unshackled and preserved from anyone who might attempt to change him or affect him.

III

The news of what had happened to Bob Long was everywhere in Danville. There would be barely anyone in the small town who hadn't heard it; only Bob's retired parents, who'd been in Europe for two weeks on a cruise ship as it slowly made its way around the boot of Italy. They would communicate with no one while they travelled, which was their custom.

At first Bob's phone rang constantly along with his front doorbell, and there were times when he heard knocking at the windows. Hour after hour the commotion didn't stop until he'd shut down his phone and posted a large sign on the front door. "Please Do Not Disturb" it said in large, black letters. People continued to approach the house during the day and evenings. Sometimes he could hear familiar voices and see the messages that dropped through his mail slot in a rising heap.

IV

Bob's body suffered more than any of his clothing. A storm of pressured blood raced though his veins with reckless force. All of his inner liquids, heated fats, and trembling nerves and muscles danced with misery and terrifying stress.

"What the hell is wrong?" his body might have cried at first. "For God's sake let us know what's happening!" Day after day there was hysteria in Bob from head to toe.

His skin itched badly. He had stopped shaving, and the lower surface of his face was sprouting stubble. One molar in his mouth had lost a filling. The tooth was throbbing in his cheek, and yet he didn't feel it. His ears, which used to hear a world of noise, were often deafened by the sounds he made. There was a table he'd upended and a chair he'd thrown against a mirror. A siege of breakage and destruction sometimes filled the air, accompanied by his choking words, and all the moans, the cries and howls that echoed through the rooms.

His eyes continually swam in tears. Each time they tried to see, they found themselves once more befogged, although Bob lost all thirst and barely drank a drop. Perhaps he'd soon be so dehydrated that he'd be devoid of fluids. There was no knowing what would happen next, and yet his eyes kept waiting on him. Swollen red, they were at his beck and call, and his entire body gave itself completely up to him, expressing every nuance of emotion that went through him, as it had never done in all the years since he was a newborn. No one could stop it.

His nose was chafed and sore. The mucous flowing through it seemed unending. Even now he was sniffing up another clod of it to spit into the toilet. His appetite was gone. It was as though he had no stomach; only nausea and sharp headaches that came and went all day.

His mouth was constantly distorted and misshapen by the changing tones and features of his grief. When he threw himself down on his bed, sometimes his heart began a brutal pounding at his ribs, as though it knew exactly what had happened. His throat became so dry and tight, he couldn't swallow and his breath so short that he felt faint. His ankles ached because he stood or paced for hours at a stretch and couldn't bring himself to sit. Some days his ankles hurt so badly, they surprised him.

V

Beyond Bob's body and his clothing, the rooms around him looked rebuffed, forsaken, and abused. The long front hall was beaten down by heavy footsteps. One floorboard had begun to splinter from repeated blows. Bob stomped his feet against the wood as he moved back and forth, hitting his fists along the walls until the plaster crumbled. The kitchen counters and the sink were riddled with old food and dirty dishes. Across the blue linoleum were remnants of a drinking glass he'd hurled and smashed to pieces on the floor.

At six p.m. one night, Bob seemed to reach a pinnacle of ruin. As he stood trembling in the living room, his limp ankles gave out and his body collapsed backwards till he slumped across the couch. His head sank down into a pillow, his eyelids shut, and then, like someone dead, he couldn't move. He had no choice about it. His pallid face went blank, and he slept so deeply that he thought of nothing in the world. His wife, Michelle, and their young children Jack, Rosetta, and Cecile were obliterated from his mind at last, as though he had been with them in the car just at the moment when the squealing, long delivery truck lost all control, broke through the guardrail on the parkway leading into Danville, hitting the white Toyota so fiercely and directly that the small car was crushed flat against the road and in an instant all its occupants were killed.

When he rose stiffly in the morning light that never

failed to reappear, Bob's feet propelled him to the up-stairs bathroom where he relieved himself. He was silent, hearing the noisy splash of his own urine and the loud flush of the toilet in the leaden quiet of the house. When his hands undid the buckle of his belt and the button at his waist above his open fly, his pants dropped to the floor. His fingers worked at his shirt buttons and untied his shoes, which he removed. With little noise his socks and underwear came off till he stood naked by the fallen heap. One knee rose as he stepped into the tub and bent down to adjust the spigot, letting the water strike his leg until he steadied himself and stood on balanced feet, closing the shower curtain with one pull. Water poured against his shoulders, drenched his hair, and when he turned around, it bathed his lidded eyes. In his hand Bob held a bar of soap. His upraised face was motionless for minute after minute while his body stood abandoned and unwashed.

VI

Bob couldn't bring himself to speak with anyone. His parents were the only people that he planned to see. Throughout the maelstrom of the past five days the date of their return had never once been lost on him. He thought of meeting them with dread. They were due to arrive home from their trip the following morning, and he was determined that he and no one else would tell them what had happened.

Bob Long had never seen his father cry or show a sign of fear. While he showered himself, shaved, put on fresh clothes, and combed his hair, it was as if his mind could fix on nothing but his parents. That night at 4 a.m. he walked the two miles to their house along dark streets of sleeping households, and with his copy of their front door key he let himself into his childhood home. The round door handle felt just as it always had as he unlocked it. Without turning on the lights he made his way across the lengthy living room and sat down on his father's arm chair, as though his senses were entirely estranged and numbed to all of the familiar smells and well-known objects in the room around him. For an hour, while he sat completely stiff and upright, taking shallow breaths, his mind seemed to be frozen on his mother and his father, as though they had become as much a part of him as his own arms and legs. He could see his father's balding head, the warm, delighted eyes that would light up in the morning, like his mother's, the moment that they opened the front door and saw him, before it could occur to them that something must be wrong to find him there.

At last Bob let out a low cry, as if he needed to release the fear that beat against his insides in repeated waves while he imagined his parent's faces listening to his news, as though the shock and horror they had never let him see in all his life might make them seem unrecognizable to him, as much as if they had become two strangers.

Memory

When I was two years old, I fell down a steep attic staircase, hitting my head against an iron radiator on the floor below. I have no memory of the accident, but my mother sometimes mentioned it, describing her terror. Blood gushed from the wound with such a fierce abundance, there was a moment when she thought it wouldn't ever stop. Both of our clothes were drenched, and the wooden floor was streaked with red. She used to say she'd never realized till that day just how much blood is hidden right beneath a person's smooth, unbroken skin. Even now an inch-long scar runs from my hairline to the center of my forehead, and for all I know there may be other lasting repercussions from that childhood fall.

I am a cautious woman: not a risk-taker. People have called me timid. They've said I'm too soft hearted, the way I never want to hurt an ant, a fly, or anything alive. And I'm a worrier as well.

※ ※ ※

There is a day I can't forget. I see the details of it clearly while thousands of other days in my sixty years alive have disappeared. I remember myself standing in a long line on Election Day outside the firehouse on Clinton Street. The questions on the ballot and the candidates for office had made it seem a crucial year to vote. My husband, Steve, was ill with a bad cold, in bed at home running a temperature. Our daughter, Lucy, wasn't old enough to vote. She had just started high school and already seemed obsessed with getting into college. She'd always been a serious student, who wasn't happy if her grades weren't good. That week she'd broken down and wept at the amount of homework she was faced with. She'd looked frightfully pale and tired, like an imprisoned person, deprived of any outdoor light. This was the way I had begun to view her schooling.

"No pain, no gain," she used to say when I urged her not to overwork herself. A soccer coach had given her that rule, as though her state of mind had no importance. At everything she did, she tried to do her best. Even her handwriting was perfect. When she wrote someone a thank-you note, not a word was ever crossed out or illegible.

※ ※ ※

That day there was a crowd of people in the voting line. It was early afternoon, yet the sky was turning dark, and I, myself, was overcome with a harsh sadness. Just after lunch I'd learned that the branch library where I'd worked for fifteen years would be shut down within three months and I'd be terminated from my job. The whole library system was due for enormous cuts, lay-offs, and massive changes. There'd been such rumors for the past two years, but now decisions had been made, and the truth clutched tightly at my stomach. I'd loved the work, my co-workers, and was so fond of many of our patrons, I couldn't imagine life without this job. Also, I worried about the loss of income, which our family needed.

When Jean Ginsberg announced the news to a room filled with my colleagues, my hand flew to my mouth, I grabbed my purse and walked out of the library shaking my head, like someone saying "no" a hundred times. I hurried to the parking lot and drove away as quickly as I could. After a few miles, I stopped beside the Parker School, where I got out and walked around the track two times and managed not to think. Then I remembered the importance of voting that day and drove across town to the firehouse. I'd forgotten my phone at home, and had a mental picture of it on the kitchen table where I'd left it. I was glad that Steve and Lucy didn't know about my miserable news.

❧ ❧ ❧

For twenty minutes at least I stood in that slow-moving line. I recognized two neighbors at a distance and waved to them, but most of the people were strangers, as one might expect to find in a large city. I remember the woman in front of me turning to face me. We exchanged comments about the weather and the threatening-looking sky. Neither of us had thought to bring umbrellas although a heavy rain had been predicted for late afternoon. We spoke of the size of the turnout, and noticed the growing line behind us. She asked me where I lived and told me her address. We didn't talk about the questions on the ballot or the candidates, whose advocates were standing on the curb behind us, waving placards.

"I've lost my job", I thought each time I took a breath. At the same time I noticed the heavy make-up on the woman's face, her nervous manner of speaking, and I wondered how she could be comfortable in her sharply pointed shoes. Finally, she faced forward, and for a while I could concentrate on nothing but the memory of Jean Ginsberg's voice and the news that kept reverberating through me.

⚜ ⚜ ⚜

I became focused on a man ahead of me in line. There were perhaps eight people standing in between us. His hair was greying, but he looked extremely fit, was nattily dressed, and talking in a lively voice to people around him. I remember it surprised me to feel how much I instantly disliked him. The woman beside him with reddish-colored hair, I guessed to be his wife, and I had a negative reaction to her as well, though I couldn't hear a word that either one was saying. The man kept turning in line with brief comments to which others responded, often with amusement. He could have been standing on a soapbox, the way he continued to attract attention. It was evident that he took pleasure in his own observations and people's reactions to his cleverness. But what was so terrible about that, I chided myself? He wasn't hurting anyone. In fact he looked intelligent, as though he might be someone highly educated, who'd been successful in his life. And yet the man continued to annoy me. I was grateful that my eyes were hidden by sunglasses so no one could see the disapproval in them.

Briefly, I focused on the wife. She wore a brightly colored scarf, a wide-brimmed, yellow hat, and over her shoulder was slung an enormous handbag of the showy, designer kind meant to announce to everyone that she had money. Mainly, she was quiet, watching and reacting to her husband, not dotingly, but dutifully, I began to think, because of all the staring looks he drew.

This man was a womanizer, I decided, noticing the way his gaze lingered on the females who responded to him. Married or not, I imagined he'd known many women and carried on affairs. He was good looking by the world's standards, though his appearance hadn't the slightest appeal for me. People around him continued to smile or laugh whenever he spoke. I guessed his words were critical or cutting, that he was cultured and sophisticated with a biting wit. I could imagine him at dinner parties, wearing a smart shirt and tie, surrounded by other guests who listened to him more often than they spoke. It's never pleasant to dislike someone, and for a while I made an effort to ignore the man.

The wait went on outside the firehouse, though we approached the building slowly. "Maybe I'll never be hired again," I thought, not knowing that within a year I would be happily established in reference at our college library, which is three miles from our house. A buzz of worries circled in my head, but I kept adjusting my glasses and looking at the couple, mainly the husband. I couldn't seem to take my eyes off him. Now that I look back on it, I wonder if I didn't welcome the distraction of his presence and the way he sometimes managed to devour my attention so completely.

At last we entered the building, where our names and street addresses were confirmed and checked off from long lists that lay across six tables. Before us was a row of curtained booths, all of them occupied by voters. The woman in front of me began to sneeze repeatedly at intervals, as though she couldn't stop. She turned towards me, clutching a tissue to her nose. "I have a million allergies," she said. A child started to cry, a toddler at the back of the room. He cried with energy, and did not stop, though his father picked him up, rocked him in his arms and kissed his face with all the tenderness and determined patience of a new young parent.

I thought of my sick husband and my Lucy, who had a history exam tomorrow. She would be studying for hours. I was proud of her marks, but when I saw her stressed, it always made me ache inside. I wanted nothing more than to go home. Ten minutes longer, I told myself, and I'd be on my way. If Steve was still so feverish and Lucy grim-faced from her schoolwork, I thought I might not talk about my job tonight to anyone.

❧ ❧ ❧

Now looking back on it years later, I can examine that whole voting day without emotion just the way I can calmly survey my mother's final days alive, and the long, devastating summer after she was gone. I see myself so clearly in the line with the woman sneezing and the child crying in its father's arms, and yet what happened next is something I have never understood.

I noticed the man's wife as she entered a booth, shutting the curtain behind her. Her husband was left alone, waiting his turn. At last he had stopped speaking. He stepped away from the man behind him, and began to whistle. At first I wondered if he might be a composer. I couldn't recognize the notes I heard. He whistled more and more loudly, as though he were entirely alone at home or outdoors in the country, but not in a crowded room of city people. When I turned around, it seemed to me that everyone was staring at him. I think my mouth must have dropped open, I was so appalled by his thoughtlessness and rudeness. Surely the concentration of the voters in the booths must be disturbed. The sound he made was shrill and so invasive that I felt outraged. Why didn't someone speak to him, I asked myself? But no one did. I remember my heart began to pound, and I was aware of a soaring fury building up inside me until two words burst from my mouth. "Stop whistling!" I called out loudly, and my anger shot like an arrow of venom aimed directly at his back. In all my life I'd never shouted at a stranger.

The man went silent, and it was a shock to see the way his body jerked, as though it had been struck. He didn't turn around, and before I knew it, both of his hands flew to his stomach. To my horror, he bent forward, gasping, and began to throw up on the floor. Before him was a growing pool of vomit. His wife leapt from her booth. "Hugh!" she cried, taking his arm, but her husband couldn't stop heaving and again sent forth a spew of yellow liquid. The smell and sight of it was terrifying, and I could feel my arms and hands were trembling.

"Everyone will have to step outside," a male voice piped up loudly. "Someone has been sick." I watched as the wife moved her husband towards the exit, her hands tightly clutched around his elbow, pulling him, step by step, like a dray horse being guided by its master. He never turned to look behind him. I remember the way I stood frozen still, holding my breath until he had completely disappeared. Once they'd gone, there was a roar of voices in the room as everyone pressed towards a single doorway to escape.

"That poor man!" the woman in front of me exclaimed. She had stopped sneezing, and she looked at me, dismayed. I remember how I whirled away and hurried off without a word.

My face felt hot in front of all these witnesses who each in turn would carry off a lasting memory of a shocking scene in which I'd played an awful role.

I pushed towards the crowded doorway with my head bent forward, cringing at the clamor in my ears and the nudge of bodies pressed up close around me. No one spoke to me. Through the open door, to my surprise, I saw that it was pouring rain across the yard. People ran from the building to their cars, and when I stepped outside at last, I remember how slowly I walked under a pounding deluge all the way to where I'd parked a block away. Once, I even stopped and stood still on the sidewalk for a moment, letting the water soak my clothes and beat down on my head until my upraised cheeks were dripping and my hair stuck to my face.

❧ ❧ ❧

It is strange the way I can't recall most days of my own past, and yet there are a few that stay entirely fixed and detailed in my mind, like a burning light that never will go out.

When I got home that afternoon, I remember that I parked in the driveway, hurried up the sidewalk through the rain, and walked into our house as though it had become a shelter from the world. Steve was in the living room in his bathrobe, reading the paper. His fever was gone, and when he saw me, he jumped up. "What's happened?" he cried", looking alarmed, crossing the room, and throwing his arms around all of my wetness.

I never cry the way I did that time. Sometimes I wailed, pressing my hands against my eyes. When Lucy came in from school, I was still weeping. Steve and I were sitting on the couch. I'd told him everything. I can see our daughter on that day. There was a sketchbook in her hand, which she took everywhere she went. She'd always had a gift for drawing, and in three years she would become a dedicated artist.

"What is it, Mom?" she said in a half whisper as she stood in the doorway. Dropping her knapsack on the floor, she ran towards me and knelt down on the rug, grabbing my hand. I remember the way she stared at me, wide-eyed, biting her lip, as though my life was all that mattered.

Jim

People always claimed that Jim Lee was the happiest man they knew. They'd never met another person like him. He'd moved to Danville in his twenties, two years after his marriage. Now he was thirty-two years old, a short, slender man with neatly combed brown hair. Jim's eyes were his most striking feature. They seemed to shine, as though the world delighted him and he was pleased by everything he saw. He smiled often, laughed and talked with his fellow workers and his customers all day. In public people often stared at him and found it hard to look away. There was an innocence about Jim's face, as though he had no secrets and all of his thoughts were evident for anyone to see. When he was charmed by something that somebody said or did, or by a lovely smell or sight, he often closed his eyes and shook his head at least three times while smiling broadly. It was a habit people recognized.

If a foolish driver backed into his car and dented it, Jim looked more fascinated than upset. It was the same when someone bumped into him along the sidewalk, accidentally stepped on his toe, or if he nicked his face while he was shaving. How could a person be so strongly interested and unperturbed by life, as though it were a marvel not to know what happened next?

"Why is he so happy?" people asked his wife.

"He's always been that way," was all she said.

Jim was the meat man at Conley's Store. He drew a crowd of people to the market every day, which pleased the owner, and while he worked it seemed that he was never tired. He spoke to everyone he served and knew most of his customers by name. Jim always looked immaculate while he was on the job. He wore a white, protective jacket and an apron that was never stained or spattered. Sometimes, late in the afternoon, the flock lined up before his counter grew and stretched before him in a widening circle. But people didn't seem to mind the wait. They were a silent group, not interested in speaking with each other; only with watching Jim. They drank him in and studied everything he did, as though they longed to find a clue that would explain him. He chose and weighed their chicken breasts, stew beef, hamburger, pork chops, and any of the meats that were available to them. Sometimes the lists of customer's requests were long, and when each order was complete, Jim leaned forward to hand over his wrapped packages to the men and women waiting to lock eyes with him and feel his warmth encompass them. His eyes were luminous, and people often stared at them, as though they had been shown a mystery that had no place in ordinary life.

Two times a year Jim and his family disappeared for a week long vacation. People were often disappointed when they found him missing from the store. "I won't make my Beef Stroganoff till he comes back," someone was likely to say. "It wouldn't be as good." Others agreed that all the meat was far more flavorful and tender when Jim prepared it. It was the best meat in town, always so fresh and beautifully displayed, it seemed untainted, like the man. Some customers had shopped at Conley's market for fifteen years or more, and even when they bought no meat, they liked to glance at Jim. While he was on vacation, his face stayed with them like a photograph that came alive each time they thought of him.

A hairdresser named Lilia walked through the market every day when Jim was there, pausing at a distance until he noticed her and waved. She'd known him ever since she'd opened up her business, which was just across the street. Jim sometimes made her think of her young husband years ago, when they'd first met, and how his eyes had danced each time he saw her. Most days she showed up at the market close to noon to find a snack for lunch, and this was when she made a point of seeing Jim, as though he were inspiring, like a dose of sugar or caffeine that sent her back to work refreshed.

✦ ✦ ✦

Jim slept eight hours each night. He dreamed in black and white, and his dream began the moment his eyes closed. It was the same dream every night. He was driving his car through rain and snow on roads turning to ice. It was early morning, the sky still dark, and the roads were treacherous, requiring his full attention. He was on his way to work, and though the traffic became heavy, he saw no people in his dream. From beginning to end he was alone. He drove until he parked behind a tall, brick building, one that he had never seen in waking life. He left his car in the empty parking lot and headed up a slippery asphalt path until he stopped to unlock a heavy, metal door with a small key. Once inside the building he began to climb the stairs up to his eighth floor office. The elevator in the hall was not an option. "Out of Order" was a sign in front of it that never changed. Always, it seemed that Jim was carrying something heavy in his arms. As he climbed up through the building, he took the stairs more and more slowly, and by the time he'd reached his office door, his face was drenched with sweat. Once in the room, he dropped his burden on his desk and paused before the only window. He stood with both hands on the sill, his forehead pressed against the glass and stared down at the dim street far below until he could no longer feel his pounding heart and his panting breath had ceased.

It was the same, the same, the same. The dream continued like a film that was replayed thousands of times. Jim switched on the harsh, fluorescent lights, took off his hat and coat and hung them in the closet. By the time he'd closed the office door and settled in the chair before his desk, it was as though he barely had a body. He no longer noticed whether he was hot or cold and in the room there never was a single sound or odor the whole time he was there. All that was left of him was his mind.

What was his job in this repeated dream that had devoured all the hours of his nights? It seemed to be some preparation that was crucial. Jim read and studied, like a person looking for an answer that was irrefutable. It was as though he were about to give a speech or to be tested on a question he could never hope to answer unless his whole attention remained riveted and pressed beyond what seemed to be the limits of his everyday intelligence, like a game of chess where there could be no lazy moment leading to a foolish loss. His mind kept pounding him with questions. Each instant brought new possibilities and choices, and he was often frustrated by himself and frightened at the thought of his own limitations. Sometimes the challenge made him want to put his head down on his desk and quit. Yet Jim would not allow himself to give in to his weakness in this lonely room where no one in the world could help him but himself.

Just once in the eight hours did he pause, knowing he must be fueled with food to think more clearly. He had no sense of taste, yet suddenly his mouth and teeth and throat came into being. Still musing on the questions in his head, he removed a sandwich and an apple from his briefcase. The gray sandwich was ham and cheese and the apple was a Macintosh. There was a small, plastic bottle of water. Always, he'd forgotten to pack a napkin, and there was no dessert, although he had a sweet tooth. Without a sound Jim ate. He didn't sigh or sniff or belch. The enormous silence of the room was never broken. It took almost an hour to consume the food. His mind remained fixed on unending problems, and he chewed each bite exactly twenty times until the pallid apple and the sandwich had disappeared inside him. By that time the silvery water bottle was completely empty. Then Jim went on with utter concentration, as though he would not let himself be stopped by anything until he'd come to a conclusion.

Yet in the dream, once Jim had finished eating, a sense of worry and impatience began to interrupt his thinking. He knew his time for work was running out. The misery of this moment was the same each night. It built and built within him like a breeze that threatened to grow fierce. At last he brought his fist down on the desk repeatedly until he realized that he couldn't feel or hear the blows he pounded on the wood. The office remained black and white and silent, as if there were nobody present in the room.

When his alarm went off, Jim felt his eyes fly open. No matter what the time of year or weather, he was always startled by the blaze of colors in his bedroom and the din of noise filling his ears. The shock was such that in an instant he forgot his dream. It disappeared as quickly as a popped balloon, and his mind appeared to be swept clean of any clue or remnant of the night. Like a dead man come to life, he found himself alone in bed. Sometimes his mouth dropped open. The morning sun was often blinding, and a world of sounds assaulted him. Many times he held his breath as he stared at the drench of yellow flowers papering the walls, the blue mirror over his dresser, and the plush, red rug that stretched across the floor. His bedside clock was green, and out the window he could see the trees and sky. Sometimes a truck roared down the road outside with a force that shook the house. Often he heard the wind, the cries of birds, the furnace switching on, footsteps along the hall, a slamming door, or a flushed toilet. The cacophony was different every morning. Then, as his head cleared, his awakened senses quickly calmed and joined together in a unison of rapture that was familiar.

His wife slept in a room next door to his because her husband sighed and tossed, talked in his sleep and snored so much that she could never rest beside him. Often, when Jim awoke, he heard her stirring from her bed. Soon his children scampered down the hall, a boy of six and a girl of four in their nightclothes.

"Papa!" they called as they burst in, jumped on his bed, and threw their arms around him, wanting to see his morning smile. Jim never disappointed them. "Oh, what a day!" he cried, kissing their warm, silky faces, while their little bodies rested on him, bursting with talk, and soon he jumped up from the bed.

Often his wife entered the room. She never knew how beautiful she looked to him in her pink robe. "Good morning, darling!" Jim said in a ringing voice, and he was rarely satisfied until he'd held her tight against him, breathing in her special fragrance with renewed appreciation. "What a day!" he'd sometimes say again, expressing his amazement.

The family separated to dress themselves, and while Jim shaved, the smell of coffee rose up from the kitchen, and he often felt his appetite grow huge. He was grateful that he'd soon eat breakfast, and as he thought of this, each moment seemed to offer a new pleasure, and all of life called to him like a welcome. Shutting his eyes and smiling as he stood before the mirror, he sometimes shook his head at least three times, and for those instants while he glimpsed the darkness under his closed lids, it was as though he longed to send his happiness like an answer to the questions he would not remember until he lay down on his bed that night and slept.

WINDS AND BIRDS
AND HUMAN VOICES

I

Henry Baron has been at the hospital for more than thirty years, like me. But I never set eyes on him till last New Year's Eve when they brought him onto this ward. I pitied him at first. His face is bandaged up. He hasn't much of a face. One bullet got him in the larynx, too. He hasn't spoken since the war. He can't walk either. His legs are no good. He is able to wheel himself in his chair, but often I push him on our daily walks when we go long distances or up hills. He's very frail, a small man like me, but terribly thin. They ought to give him therapy, some exercises to build him up, his strength. But they don't. Till he met me he stayed in bed most of the day. They bathed him and they fed him. They changed his bandages. Beyond that they ignored him. Of course, they've given up on all of us "chronics" on this psychiatric ward.

I noticed that Henry (or "the Baron", as I sometimes call him) had no visitors. He appeared to be completely abandoned. For this I also pitied him. My mother, my brother Bill and sister Kathleen came to see me when they could. My father couldn't come. It was too painful for him. But while he was alive, I saw him off and on when I felt up to going home for certain holidays.

I was drawn to Henry from the start. I'd pass his room and see him lying there alone and still hour after hour. More often than not, he was weeping silently, the tears streaming down across the bandaged face, with no one there to comfort him. The sight of him was disturbing. You don't see tears on our ward. You may see rage or violence, but you don't see tears. The men passed that point years ago. But the Baron's grief seemed sharp and fresh, as though he'd had some recent loss or shock. Sometimes he appeared to weep for days, and the sign of his loneliness and suffering was so forlorn, it made me sick at heart. The nurses hardly seemed to notice him. They drank their coffee, laughed and gossiped at their station. You could see they didn't give a damn.

I began to visit him. I'd sit in the chair beside his bed and I'd talk to him. He wouldn't make a sound, but I'd know that he was listening. How I knew this, I can't say. He lay completely still and didn't give a single sign, but I knew he heard me. I stopped to see him every day, and when I was with him, I noticed that his tears stopped. After about a week, he began to squeeze my hand or nod his head to show he understood. This excited me a great deal. In fact, I felt triumphant. The more he responded the more I felt compelled to stay with him. Sometimes I'd spend the entire day beside his bed talking. I told him everything about myself. Often I wondered how there could be so much to tell of such an empty, repetitious life. But always there was more to add. At first it hardly seemed to matter what I said. Henry listened to it all, his head tipped back so I could see the shapeless hollow of his profile where his cheek was blown away.

He drank in every word I said, as if he had a thirst and all my rambling hours of talk were a shower that rained down on him and revived him. A few times I gave the Baron pencil and paper to see how he would answer certain questions. He had great trouble writing. One day it took him five minutes to print the word 'yes'. I could hardly read his handwriting it was so bad. But I knew he understood me, every word I said, even if he couldn't put his own thoughts into words. I could tell by the way he shook with laughter at the jokes I told him. (I told him every joke I knew one day.) Or the way he'd sigh or smile, depending on the story, always in tune with what I said.

Our ward is an open ward, which means that the patients are free to leave the building so long as they fill out the sign-out sheet with the time, the destination, and the hour of return. I was the one who got Henry out of bed and took him out-of-doors. It was the first time he'd been outside in years. I could see that he was delighted. It wasn't long before he wanted to go out every day regardless of the weather.

The hospital grounds are enormous. They are gorgeously planted and meticulously gardened. Never have you seen such giant, spreading elms that look like great explosions in the air, or such luxurious lawns of grass so darkly green and thick. There are so many paths, long lanes planted with rows and rows of flowers, all of them perfect. You never see a dead one. "Think of the expense," I've said to Henry. "And who is it for?" Most of the patients never leave the buildings. When we take our daily walks, we rarely see a soul. I push the Baron ahead of me in his chair. His eyes are as good as mine. There is nothing wrong with his hearing or sense of smell. He enjoys the view the same as I do.

A change came over me as I began to spend my time with Henry Baron. I no longer played cards with the day nurse, Mrs. Cooley. Nor did I shoot the breeze with the attendant, Arthur Little, who'd used to walk the corridors with me and smoke, discussing baseball games and football scores nights when I couldn't sleep. I stopped talking to everyone but Henry. When I was asked a question, I didn't answer it. Mrs. Cooley kept after me at first, and Arthur made it difficult, too. "What's the matter, Paul?" they'd say. "Are you angry? Are you depressed?" But after awhile they let me be.

It was a relief to talk to no one but the Baron. It was such a relief that I wrote a letter to my family and told them not to visit me for a while. I knew my brother Bill would be happy to receive this news. He'd just been made the president of his company. The more successful he's become, the harder it's been for him to visit me. In his three-piece suit and his white Mercedes he arrives, his hair still thick and tousled, but now grey, his face a mask of shame when I ask about his work, his pretty wife Melina, who sends me cards for every holiday, and their three children, one of whom is named for me. Bill thinks I must be envious of him. My mother, frail and in her seventies, would be spared the hour of strain in the hospital, a nightmare world through which she walked with carefully averted eyes. Behind her smile, I always felt the misery of her love escape and float across to me as strong as her perfume. My sister Kathleen, who lives nearby, two towns away, is a social worker, recently divorced from her husband Michael after twenty years. They were never able to have children, which is the disappointment of Kathleen's life. She's over-worked and haggard looking now. Her face is colorless and deeply lined. No matter how fond she's always been of me, I knew she, too, would feel released when I told her I wasn't up to having visitors.

I hadn't known him long before I sensed that Henry and I were kindred creatures with a surprising amount in common. Not just two mental patients bound by our afflictions. I believed that he had been and continued to be a man of sophistication and intelligence. It is intriguing how much you can learn about a man without his ever uttering a word. I sat beside his bed. The sun shone on the white spread, the stiff sheets, and on his hands which lay at his sides with the palms turned up as if to catch the light. The Baron's hands always surprised me. They seemed so large for a man his size. The fingers were long and tapering, delicate and white, the hands of a philosopher or an artist. While I spoke, he listened, staring at the ceiling. Sometimes when he turned to look at me there was such sympathy in his eyes, I felt I could see the whole expression of his face beneath the bandages. Our friendship had changed him, too. He no longer wept. Some nights, sensing he was awake, I slipped down the hall to check on him. Often I found him gazing out the windows at the moonlit sky. But he seemed completely calm and I felt as proud as if his mood were my accomplishment. In fact I saw a vast improvement in him, a rising of his spirits, and an exuberance that seemed to build, as though he were coming more to life each day. He looked forward to our walks with an eagerness that touched me. Out of doors on a particularly pretty afternoon or evening when the air was pulsing with bird cries or drifting with the fragrance of pine or flowers or fresh mown grass, he would sometimes stop the chair, throw up his hands and hold them up or out in front of him as if he couldn't contain his enthusiasm and would have liked to embrace the whole view for all the beauty he saw in it. Whenever he did this, I felt a peculiar stab of pain, as if the memory of joy, of fearless and ecstatic praise were more than I could bear: I, who always expected the worst.

I saw that Henry was a passionate man. He reminded me of myself, the person I'd used to be so long ago that I could hardly call it myself any longer. I was certain that his rapture would not last, that the novelty of my company and the out-of-doors would wear out. Then, having tasted happiness, I would sure he would, like all men, be hungry for more. But how much could the Baron hope for? What kind of a life? I expected that eventually, any day now, he would fall into a cavernous depression. I told myself I'd regret that I had ever spoken to him. But I continued to see him every day.

In the spring we started to play chess. In the morning we'd have a game, usually in Henry's room. He never liked to sit in the dayroom. The sight of other patients pacing or babbling to themselves or staring off in space depressed him. I was surprised he hadn't gotten used to it. Also, the television, which is always on. The sound of it got on his nerves. And the bad air. Even in summer with the windows open, there is a strong smell, a sour human smell. Not to mention all the cigarette smoke. Back then the patients were allowed to smoke. Being a smoker myself, it never bothered me. But Henry was always happiest when we were by ourselves and out-of-doors. As the weather grew warmer, we took our game outside. There was a picnic table under a large maple tree at the back of our building. The Baron sat in his chair. I sat on the bench across from him, and no one ever bothered us. If I'd had any doubts about the Baron's mind or whether his reasoning ability had been impaired, they were put to rest when I saw him play chess. He was a slow but ingenious player, with enormous concentration. There wasn't a move he made that wasn't deeply calculated, and in the end he always trounced me.

Often I'd stop in the middle of a game and go up to the building to fetch two Cokes from the machine. The smallest things delighted Henry. He gave me the feeling that playing chess and drinking Coke and sitting across from me under the open sky were all that he wanted in the world. When he leaned across the table, shook my arm, and smiled with all-out pleasure, it was as if he had no memory of suffering or injury, as if he had no past at all. It was strange how much his happiness, even the smallest evidence of it, affected me with pride, anxiety and even fear, and the more inseparable we became, the more I seemed to feel the power of his personality as if it were the atmosphere I breathed.

One afternoon, after Henry had played a brilliant game, we stayed at the table. The day was warm and the air so fresh it rose and danced for miles above, as if the winter sky had been a heavy roof that now was lifted. There was a soaring, endless feeling to the air. His head resting on one hand, Henry gazed at the view. His eyes appeared to be completely serene. I found myself staring at him, wondering what his problem was and why they'd put him on the psychiatric ward. There's little mystery about our chronics. Most of them have been here for years. You know their fears and their obsessions as well as you'd know a normal man's opinions. I stared at Henry. His physical disability, his deformity was obvious, but other than his initial fits of weeping, I'd seen no sign of his psychosis. Not once in the five months he'd been on the ward. Of course, I, too, had been unusually well the whole time I had known him. I wondered if, like me, his illness had a cycle. Like me and Ben Dimento, who fought in Viet Nam. My cycle used to be as regular as Ben's. Six months of perfect health, six months of hell. Like clockwork. The doctors used to study me. I'd read about myself in psychiatric journals. I wondered if the Baron was like me, if even now behind that calm façade he felt the signs and subtle stirrings of his illness, as if it were a hibernating giant, half-roused by sounds and smells of spring. There wasn't a summer since the war when I hadn't been completely mad.

I studied Henry closely, whose upturned face still looked so satisfied. I thought of the way he relied on me more and more. He waited for me anxiously each morning. When I appeared he took my arm with pleasure and relief. His growing dependence was flattering, but it worried me, sometimes to the point where my hands trembled when I thought of it. When Henry noticed the trembling, he took my hands in his and held them until the shaking stopped. He took my hands so naturally and with such ease, there was no embarrassment in it. I felt that I must warn him and prepare him for the worst, but I couldn't bring myself to do it yet.

II

When I think of my past, the early happy years are another life, a story that came to an end as final and complete as death. The child I was is a stranger about whom I know everything, a boy named Paul who showed an interest in the piano. When he'd come in from school, this little Paul would go straight to the livingroom, which in the afternoon was orderly and hushed. The sun poured silently through gleaming windows down on the spotless yellow carpet, and the air was faintly scented with his father's pipe tobacco. He'd pass the flowered couch, the tables rubbed with lemon oil to shining, and slide across the slippery bench before the looming upright Steinway whose heavy ivory keys lay waiting, faintly yellowed to a color that seemed sanctified with mystery and beauty. Often he'd start to play with his hat and coat still on and stay there till his mother ordered him outside for an hour of fresh air. When he was six, he started lessons, and from that moment was so enchanted and possessed that had he been allowed he would have done nothing else but play. In the evenings after dinner he'd go back to practice. His father, if he were at home, would puff his pipe and read in his high-backed chair across the room. "That's *wonderful*, Paul," he'd sometimes say with real surprise. He had no musical ability himself and was slightly awed by the reports of the piano teacher, Adele Archer, who said she'd never had a pupil with such promise. His mother, too, was pleased, but not surprised. She seemed to expect her children would do wonders and was only amazed when they were rude or bad.

He learned to play his little Bach and Mozart pieces easily and practiced them until the lurching notes smoothed together and rang out proudly from his hands. By the time he was eight he began to give recitals with several of Miss Archer's other pupils. He sat before a crowd without the slightest nervousness or fear, and while he played a silence louder than applause would build within the room inspired by the confidence and natural bravado with which the child performed.

Throughout those early years Miss Archer's long horse face appeared to be continually wreathed with admiration. At their weekly lessons she listened to him play, her hands clasped tightly to her chest, as if a miracle were happening in her living room. "It is *astonishing* the way he picks up everything so quickly," she told his parents in a voice that nearly trembled, her face becoming radiant when she looked down at her kindled student whose future rose before her like the sun. "I've been waiting for a child like Paul for thirty years," she said.

Something about Adele Archer's flushed cheeks, the long strands of her hair which came unpinned in her excitement and hung loosely by her face, disturbed the father. The careless look of her clothes, the way her skirt hung on her bony frame, and the surprising feeling in her naked eyes, gave her a starved, unhealthy look. "I worry about that woman," he'd sometimes say to the mother in a burst of impatience. "I think she's pushing the boy too hard."

But it wasn't Miss Archer who drove Paul to practice longer and longer hours. It was the music, the subtlety and the difficulty of which steadily increased, as if he'd been continually climbing, had passed the easy foothills and now found himself upon a startling slope which rose up with a steepness that required all of his skill. By the time he was twelve he began to dream of mountains, soaring alps which stretched before him in a chain of glory all the way to the horizon. The farthest peaks towards which he struggled were lost in clouds of unimaginable beauty.

One night, after a recital, Dr. Winslow, a friend of his father's, came up to congratulate him. "Tell me, Paul. What would you do if you couldn't play the piano anymore?" he said with a teasing smile. The question hung in the air while the child's face twisted with confusion. "I would die," he said at last, and he saw his own dismay reflected in the doctor's face.

Paul liked it best to practice in the summer, sunny days when his mother opened all the windows and the out-of-doors hummed like a great machine. From where he sat he had a view of his mother's terraced garden. Often she worked with her flowers or his father would appear at the door of the tool shed, the sun flashing in his glasses, and a world of sounds and smells rode through the room. He played to the noise of voices, footsteps, birds, and the steady whine of insects, as if the sounds of summer were his orchestra. And when he played his best, he disappeared into the music, drifted on the notes right out the window of the lonely room into the brilliant summer yard, rose above the buildings, moved in the heavy-laden trees, or wafted out across the grass with an intensity that made his mother put her trowel down and turn to stare at the dark empty window.

After summer came dim afternoons when rain pelted the windows and the wind blew hard and wild outside while the room remained untouched. And winter days when the sky was a heavy, shifting veil of grey and the snow descended hour after hour, steadily and slowly, until the piano sounded loud and harsh in the vast accumulating silence. There were evenings when his concentration built like such an all-surrounding wall, it was a great relief to turn away from the piano, to find his mother knitting on the couch behind him, to see the colors of her sweater, pink or mauve or emerald green, and all the colors of the room leap forward like a welcome. He'd rise with a feeling of exhaustion, go to sit by his mother's feet, rest his head against her knee, and stare into the cheerful, blazing fireplace like a traveler returning from a distance. He'd stare at the steadfast lamps and chairs and tables, feel the warmth of the fire and of his mother's love which flowed through the hand she placed on his shoulder, and he'd stay there till the sense of lostness and separateness had passed.

Already he'd felt the power of his mind, the way it could bewitch and hold him captive, lost to the world while his hand ran up and down the keys, enchanted little hands that moved so freely of their own volition. And the more he disappeared into the music, the more important grew the moment when he'd turn away from the piano to face the solid beauty of the room. He came to count upon the impact of the room as if it were a healing blow that broke a spell releasing him from his mind back to the world. Years later, when he'd come home for a weekend visit, when he'd wander through the house as if he needed to inspect the rooms, he would avoid the livingroom. Home from the hospital for a long weekend, he'd climb the staircase to the second floor, follow the trail of rugs along the hall and stop at each open bedroom door. He'd tour the grounds, pause by his mother's garden, pass through the long dark dining room into the commotion of the kitchen or sit long hours on the veranda or the porch. But he never would go near the living room. The family was sure it must be the piano he avoided, that the sight of it was devastating to him. But they were wrong. It wasn't the piano, but the livingroom itself he couldn't bear to see, because it, too, had lost all impact, any power to bring him back, and now appeared like all the world to be a dream.

III

I have no memories of the war. Perhaps the heavy drugs I've taken have destroyed them. Whole years are gone as if they had been bombed into oblivion. I'm told that I saw action only for six months and that my company was at Anzio when I was declared mentally incompetent and unfit and shipped home to a psychiatric hospital. I remember little of the two years I spent at Glenside Hospital. Only that I was disoriented and that my doctors discouraged me from playing the piano because it caused me too much stress. I was told that my prognosis was good and that with patience, time, and rest I would recover. I never believed this. In fact my weekend visits home convinced me I was growing steadily worse. I was twenty and I saw the world with the detachment and nostalgia of a dying man. All the most normal events and common sights developed poignancy and power. A table set for five became poetic. An easy chair, a rug, a pair of shoes, the faithful stars, the rising sun all developed extra meaning and importance. The world became a place of shining warmth within which normal people lived entirely immersed. I'd see them walking down the street at home with every shape or shade of color, temperature or change of weather, basking in familiar sounds and smells, unsurprised by anything. I'd see the way these people blindly ate their meals, conversed and sipped their drinks or calmly slept with an acceptance that made all human weaknesses and failings appear harmless and endearing for the innocence implied by such enormous faith, a faith which made a man belong entirely to the world the way a thoughtless tree belongs. While I, as I become more ill, become more outcast, saw all life with a clarity and distance that shattered innocence, with the loneliness of a voyeur who feels the shame of his detachment, as if it were the greatest sin of all. Sometimes I was so overcome with consciousness that I could not remember how to hold a fork or walk across a room with any ease or grace.

❦ ❦ ❦

Each summer there is a day when a trumpet blast cuts through the air. Then, if I strain my ears, I can hear the faintest sound of beating drums, the distant tramp of soldier's feet, and the rattle of their sabers. I can hear an army marching far away, but on its way to me. It is a sound which used to chill my blood. In the early years I'd pace the floor for weeks while the steady tramp of feet grew louder. I'd moan, I'd cry, I'd pull my hair and beat my head against the floor until they'd have to put restraints on me. "Save me," I'd beg the orderlies and nurses. They'd look at me with pity and they'd drug me heavily, but nothing stopped the pounding feet which grew continually louder. Sometimes I passed out from the strain or fell into a swoon of fear on the hard floor. I'd see the hospital for days bathed in a brilliant shade of pink, then darkening to an ever deeper red until the nurses and the patients all began to fade slowly and horribly. At last they disappeared in darkness.

Each year this sequence of events repeats itself with a hundred variations. Once the hospital has faded out I remain in a darkness more profound and deep than any in the living world. The stomp of feet is deafening by now and the rat-tat-tat of drums. I wait for the moment of total silence which comes just at the instant when I least expect it, that moment when the drums cease, when the feet come to a sudden halt, and when there is a rolling, awesome quiet more powerful than any sound. How long this pregnant silence lasts, this final moment of transition, I can't say. I wait in that hopeless blackness which is timeless.

Some years, at the boom of a single cannon, a scene completely formed bursts into a bloom of color all around me. I'm sure I'll never know the meaning of this stark, familiar scene, this panoramic grand display of symbols crucial to my soul. I stand at the edge of a skeletonic forest which has been entirely destroyed by fire. Before me lies a scorched field two miles wide which rises to a distant pointed ridge. All across this lifeless field the grass is blackened to the ground. No birds appear here, no brave surviving squirrel roots in the broken stubble of the forest. Not even the lowest insect lives or moves in this still landscape. I search the view, hoping to find some hole in it, some weakness of imagination which will make it less believable. But everything I see is starkly real and rendered perfectly down to the last detail of distance and perspective. The more I look, the more the overwhelming authenticity of the scene wraps and seals itself around me in such a way that there is no escape.

Some years I see the army marching toward me over that conquered field with all the glamour of a history painting come to life in the smoky, hazy light. I see how antiquated their weapons are, all their swords, their cannons and equipment, as if this army had defeated time itself. The faces of the men are hard and white, their uniforms a brilliant red with yellow tassels at the shoulders, fringe along the sleeves. The boots they wear are shiny, black and high.

Sometimes I see the General himself who leads them on a skittish, prancing horse, his thick straight hair tossed back from his enormous, chiseled face, his eyes steeling and harsh above a twisted cruel mouth. He rarely speaks to me as he approaches. He doesn't need to speak. He leads his men into my consciousness each summer. He plants the flag of his possession deep and makes my mind his camping place.

Some years ago I never see the men at all, but I know exactly how they look. The taste of them is like the taste of metal in my mouth. And it is suffering, pain enough to feel the bruising touch of all their striding, heedless feet. A mind is sacred ground. You cannot know this till the moment of a great invasion. You cannot know the awful pressure or the frightful strain as the men file in, toss all their weapons down and the heavy weight of their equipment. Yet still they keep arriving, pressing in until there isn't any inch of empty space left in me, and the tidal sound of them, the roaring chaos and the grand confusion of them rises to a pitch that shatters my last desperate concentration. Then I am nothing. I am theirs.

When I was first at Washington V.A., I used to fight each onset of my illness. At the sound of the trumpet blast in June, I picked up chairs and heaved them all the way across the dayroom. I broke windows. I put my fist through the television screen. The more I fought the more enormous my strength grew. One year I took on the whole cafeteria. I threw plates and trays. I flipped the trestle tables over and I flung them in the air light as balloons. I picked up cups and smashed them one by one against the ceilings, floors and walls. No one could stop me. It took six orderlies to bring me down. They had to lock me in a padded cell from June through Christmas. I was a holy terror in those days. But the army was equally impressive. The men were young, invincible, and fierce. They had no wounds or scars or any sign of weakness. Their uniforms were new and spotless, made of such a brilliant red it hurt the eyes to look at them.

They spoke to me. For half the year I heard their voices, loud and scornful, cold and haughty, or soft and silky and insinuating. Sometimes they spoke to me in choruses, in waves, and sometimes singly, individually using whatever tone was most effective at the time. I lay on a mat on the floor of my padded cell. The walls were white. One naked bulb hung down protected by a wire cage eight feet above. Their voices, dark and predatory, circled me, and in those days there was no end to the havoc they could cause.

Two weeks before my father died, he tried to visit me. Maybe he had a premonition of his heart attack. My mother drove up to the hospital with him. They came one afternoon just after lunch. The doctors wouldn't let them see me. I was far too ill for visitors, they were told. Of course, nobody let me know that my parents had arrived. I was sitting in a chair on the ward, staring off in space, when something made me rise and walk across the room to the right window. I looked down at the parking lot and was surprised to see my father and mother walking to their car. It was warm. The window was barred, but it was open. I was going to call down to them. I was just about to when I saw my father stop. His face was in his hands. He was bent over, and my mother put her arm around his waist. She seemed to be supporting him. They looked so small, I felt I could have picked them up and held them in my hand. The cloudless sky was blue and vast above them and for just that moment I could truly see what I had done to them. Many times I have imagined and replayed this scene. My parents are in the parking lot with all the joy, the life gone out of them, and I am at the high-barred window unable to call down to them. Did it ever really happen? I am never sure.

Some rare cool-headed nights when I was in my twenties, I used to lie in the purest, soothing darkness of my room at 3 a.m. and glory in the silence of the hospital, which seemed to match the quiet of my mind when sanity and privacy had been restored to it. In such a mood of gratitude I'd sometimes have to climb out of my bed, to walk about my room and feel the floor unshakeable and steady under my bare feet. I'd have to touch the metal bed post, to run my hand over the smooth-painted wall, to touch the light switch and to think that if I turned it on I'd see exactly what I would expect to see and nothing more. Sometimes the pleasure and the gratitude were so intense, I'd have to leave my room and step into the lighted hall where the shiny, checked linoleum was all that I saw or wanted to see and where the smudged green walls, the high grey ceilings and the iridescent lights above all waited unobtrusively and humbly, not caring whether I noticed them or not. By four a.m. over the whole ward the silence had a texture thick as soil. On nights like this I'd ask myself the meaning of my madness the way a normal man might hope to understand the stars or wonder at a stretch of strange, unseasonable weather, as if there had to be some explanation for it. I'd study my own illness with the coldness of a scientist who prides himself on his detachment. I'd ask myself the meaning of the General and the significance of the antiquated army. Why did they come specifically in June, and what was the reason for the six-month cycle? Those brave, light-headed nights I'd feel quite sure that if I solved these riddles, my dread army would disintegrate and disappear forever. I'd be cured. But I never found a single answer to my questions. One thing only was clear, that the army's purpose was the purpose of all armies: to demoralize and to defeat the enemy, which was me.

❧ ❧ ❧

My mother came to see me every year just after Christmas. "How are you, dear?" she'd ask, touching my cheek. "I'm fine," I'd tell her lightly, and I would produce the wide and carefree and preposterous smile I carefully prepared for every meeting with her, which by some miracle of love or mutual collusion was always effective. I saw my mother's face relax. Then we would limp through conversation. There was little to say. In the early years she brought me music scores and books: "The Principles of Composition," and heavy, hardbound lives of Rimsky-Korsakoff and Charles Ives. I never had the heart to tell her I no longer read. I'd lost the concentration for it. "Have you been practicing at all?" she'd ask me hopefully. There was a "music room" in Building 9. My first few years at Washington I sometimes practiced on the spinet in that room, though it was always out of tune. But there was never any pleasure in it. Since the war, by some odd twist of heightened nerves and over-sharp perceptions my ear had grown so piercingly acute that I could read a score and hear precisely how a piece should be interpreted down to the finest subtleties of tempo and dynamics. There was a simple Bartok piece I played for weeks hundreds of times a day and never once came close to the perfection of my ear. I went into such fits of fury and frustration banging on the keys that finally I was forbidden from further playing. Dr. Sewell must have spoken to my mother. After that she didn't bring me music anymore.

Nor books either. She brought me cartons of the Marlboros I smoke one after another all day long, which were all that I wanted.

❧ ❧ ❧

Each year, after the army had played out all of their tricks, there came a day in late December when they'd start to pack their gear. I'd watch them break camp in their slow, methodic way. This, too, was torture. It took them days and days. Each year the General came up to me as they were leaving. He came up close until his face was looming and immense. "You know the rules, Paul," was what he said. You are to keep everything you've seen and heard here to yourself. One word, one slightest hint of it to anyone and there will be *hell* to pay." Then he mounted his great horse, he whirled away from me, and he was gone. I never wondered at his power, the sinking nausea and the instant terror that the sight of him always inspired. With lips sealed tight as if they had been welded by the General's command, I watched the men file slowly out behind him. It was always raining as they disappeared over the ridge, raining on them and on the muddy ground they'd left all littered and defiled.

I tested the General once, one night of a full moon when I was in my thirties. I started to tell Mrs. Davis, the night nurse, about my army of tormentors. It was a January night. I could see the swollen moon, enormous, cold and white outside the window of my room. Mrs. Davis was leaning over me, wiping my face with a damp towel. My arms were wrapped with gauze. I'd tried to cut my wrists.

"What is it, Paul?" she said. She could see that I wanted to speak. I took her arm and held it tightly. I planned to tell her everything. And yet when I tried to find words that would describe the army's tactics, and the meaning of those long, kaleidoscopic months of nightmare images and darting scenes with which they'd held and punished and absorbed me, my mind appeared to melt into confusion.

"What is it, Paul?" said Mrs. Davis softly. "Can you tell me?" She leaned close over me, over my face which was pouring sweat.

"Try to tell me," she said gently. Her breasts just grazed my chest. I thought I heard the sound of drums begin, the steady roll and beat of them. I closed my eyes to concentrate and when I opened them I saw that Mrs. Davis was laughing. Her eyes were cruel slits and her white nurse's uniform was turning red. A cry escaped me, but it came out as a trumpet sound, long and high and shrill. I heard the General's voice beside my ear.

"I warned you, Paul," he said. I can remember Mrs. Davis's laughing face, her dress which seemed to float and shimmer red before my eyes, and how I watched her fade until she disappeared into a rising, swimming darkness. That was the last I saw of her for two years. The army kept me raving mad on the locked ward for two years as punishment for my attempted betrayal.

After I came back from that long siege, Bill was the first one in the family to visit me. When they brought me down to the visitor's room, he looked shocked. "You've lost so much weight, Paulie," he said. "You've got to eat more." I asked about Melina and the children and how his work was going. He looked uncomfortable the way he always did when he talked about himself in front of me. I wanted to say, "For God's sake, Bill, I'm so far gone you couldn't pay me to be you."

There is a crossing point after long illness when a man begins to dread the possibility of ever being well again more than the prospect of remaining permanently ill. The hospital can recognize the signs: the glassy eyes, the aimless, shifting walk, the robot voice. The empty face without a human sign or message to convey makes a powerful impression, one that might be harmful to the other, healthier patients. This is what the hospital believes and why they've made a special building for the chronics to keep them hidden separate from the others.

When I was forty-two they put me with the chronics. By then it mattered little to me where I lived or slept. In the company of those milling, babbling men who drifted up and down the corridors with the vague directness of sleepwalkers, I sank into a numb obliviousness. Sometimes I was aware that weeks and months had disappeared without my noticing, as if once time had detached from any purpose, it speeded up and rocketed like something that has been unleashed. Sometimes I watched the clock and felt the pulsing minutes flow unchecked out of my life as swiftly as the rush of blood escaping from a mortal wound.

In the dayroom we sat in chairs against the walls, a long-curved row of bodies silent and entranced. The morning sun shone on the floor. It made a yellow square unnoticed and unseen by anyone. In the center of the room a man paced back and forth. All day from his small mouth there came a steady flood of gibberish which rose and fell and was monotonously soothing like the sound of bees.

They didn't have to lock me up in summer anymore. I found this out from Arthur Little. I asked him once whether I was ever violent anymore. "Hell, no Paul. You're no trouble," he said. "When you're sick, you just sit in your chair all day. You don't talk to nobody and you don't do nothing. You're quiet as a lamb," he said. "Sometimes I walk you up and down the halls to exercise you. 'Come with me, Paul,' is all I have to say. I lead you by the arm and you come right with me. You're no trouble to nobody, Paul," he said. "No trouble at all."

❧ ❧ ❧

When I turned fifty, I noticed that the General was going grey, and I saw how much all of his soldiers had aged along with me. The company grew slightly smaller every year, and the men appeared less strong and more obviously tired. There were more wounded and more who walked with canes, who limped, and some who had lost an arm or leg. The uniforms were soiled and patched. The boots were worn. Some had no boots and walked with painful feet bound up with cloth and tape. As they approached me over the ridge, their faces were more bored than hostile towards me. They rarely spoke to me or wanted my attention. They simply occupied me now. They dressed their wounds and they rested their weary bodies. For the most part they ignored me. One year I noticed that I'd almost lost my fear of them. I even spoke to the General once and I asked him a frivolous question. "You've kept me here all of these years. You've made me suffer any way you could. One thing has always puzzled me," I said. "Why did you let me smoke all of these years? Why did you allow me that one pleasure?"

"Because it was killing you," he replied.

I actually laughed when I heard that, which seemed to dismay the general. For a moment he looked quite shaken, and there was something grotesque about the uncertainty and the frailty I clearly saw in his softened, aging face. Then his expression changed. He smiled.

"I have to admire you, Paul," he said. "You've never betrayed us all of these years." The words were flattering and yet there was a razor tone of irony and scorn in them which made me suddenly look closely at the General's face. At his mouth, which was disdainful and amused. And in his narrowed eyes I saw the confidence and calculation of a player, who far from finished, still holds a crushing trump card hidden in his hands.

My mother came to see me twice a year, just before the arrival of the army and shortly after their departure, the times I was expected to be well. I don't believe she ever knew how much I had deteriorated. Each time she came into the ward, I was ready for her, smiling brightly. The nurses must have seen how much these visits cost me. They always warned me several days before my mother came. From whatever depths of illness I had gone to, I heard the nurses' far-off, faintly spoken message, and I would stir and strain to rouse myself from that dim, muffled place of ringing emptiness where I lay hidden and protected. Perhaps it was the place all chronics went to. Then, like a swimmer under heavy weights of water, I would rise to meet my mother on the surface, though the distance and the effort of that passage seemed more onerous each year. Also, the pain. The pain of breaking through the surface into the roaring light of the dayroom where the din was overwhelming. I wondered how I ever had endured that brilliant light which bounded sharply off the walls like hurled knives aimed straight at me. And all the world's confusion and commotion. On all sides was shifting, dizzy motion. Such a blast of sharp, intruding smells. I gripped the arms of my hard chair as if I might be shaken free by all the forces in the room. I thought of Mother. I prepared myself to see her.

It was after one of Mother's visits that I first saw Henry Baron. I had walked Mother to the door and was on my way back to the dayroom full of a sense of fatigue so severe that I wondered if I could even make it to my chair. There was a farewell smile still plastered on my face as I passed Henry's room. I never paused. I continued on my way down the long corridor, and yet the image of the man I'd seen stayed right in front of me as if I'd stopped beside his door and still remained there staring at him.

IV

I arrived at Henry's room by eight o'clock each morning. He no longer liked to take his meals in bed. He enjoyed eating with me. I always found him wide awake and waiting eagerly for my arrival. His eyes lit up and shone with happiness when I appeared at his door. It is hard to describe the effect that this greeting had on me. I was not used to bringing joy to anybody. But then I was not used to any of the changes in my life since I'd known Henry. Often it seemed impossible that he was sitting across from me, that I'd just spoken to him. I kept expecting him to disappear. I was quite sure that some fine day I'd find his bed made up and empty. He'd be gone as suddenly as he'd come, and there would be no explanation for it. Perhaps the Baron had this same anxiety and that was why he greeted me with such enthusiasm every morning. He grasped my hand and held it tightly. Then I helped him into his chair and he wheeled himself down to the cafeteria where we had breakfast. While we ate, we often planned what we would do that day. In the mornings we played chess or we sat together in the sun. Hours would go by without a word or sign exchanged between us, yet there was a constant feeling of communion of a kind I'd never known with anyone before. It frightened me.

I could now sit comfortably in the morning sun. The light was soft. It wasn't painful to my eyes. I could look across the rolling lawn of shifting grass and swaying trees and passing cars without the slightest dizziness. Clouds inched across the sky, birds flew, and people walked among the buildings while I remained unmoved, perfectly still. The morning sounds of droning mowers, gardener's clippers, wind and birds and human voices seemed subdued and gentle to my ears.

I stopped playing cards with Mrs. Cooley. To sit with her seemed tiresome and pointless. In fact, all talk with anyone but Henry was annoying. When I wrote my family not to visit me, I was surprised at how pleased I felt. More amazing was the tremendous improvement in my thinking the moment I stopped speaking with the staff. The very day I broke communication with them, my concentration sharpened to a point where I came very close to beating Henry at chess. My mind was suddenly so clear that I could see the fuzzy, muddying effect that my twice-daily dose of medications had on it. I began to hide the pills they gave me underneath my tongue and to dispose of them whatever way I could. In the days that followed, as I grew increasingly alert and energetic, it came as an unpleasant shock to think that all the drugs I'd swallowed might have done more harm than good.

In the afternoons we took our walks. We headed down the path and the row of ominous brick buildings shrank behind us to the size of toys. I pushed the Baron in his chair when he grew tired. Often we went two miles to reach our favorite resting spot. At the top of a steeply winding path was a wide, sheer cliff with a spectacular view of checkered farms far down below. On a grassy knoll above the precipice someone had placed a wooden bench where you could rest and gaze out over the expanse of fields and buildings, woods and lakes, and mountains at the farthest distance. Henry always threw his arms up at the sight of this great liberating view, and I often thought that these wide gestures of his arms, the thousand signals of his delicate long hands and the sharp expression in his eyes were far more powerfully explicit than words could ever be.

Not far from our cliff view was an old abandoned chapel, a grey stone building almost hidden in a crowd of juniper and pine. The heavy door was never locked and it was easy to push the Baron's chair over the low sill. More than once we went inside and sat in the silent, oblong room of darkly varnished pews and stained class windows. The air was cut with shafts of purple, red and green and had a musty, piney smell. A wooden cross hung from the wall above the empty marble altar. As we sat in the failing light of afternoon, there was a lonely echo to the bird cries outside the building and a hollow feeling to the darkening surrounding woods which made me glad that the Baron was beside me.

By early May I felt so well, and I was convinced that all of it was my friend's doing, even the beauty of the spring and my capacity to perceive it. The sky was a blue pastel day after perfect day. In the balmy warmth and the golden light everything was in bloom. The air that breezed across the grounds was heavily perfumed with lilacs and the banks and banks of lilies, hyacinths and nasturtium which the gardeners daily tended. Beside our buildings were blonde fountains of forsythia cascading with long sprays of yellow stars. For twenty years or more I'd never noticed spring at all. This year I was intoxicated.

One shadow fell through all of this exhilaration, which was the thought of my approaching army due to arrive in six short weeks or less. They'd always been on schedule. Why wouldn't they be now? And what would Henry think when I no longer showed up in the morning, and when I sat like a vegetable in the dayroom all day long in my chair, as Arthur Little had described it. I could imagine it so well, how Henry, having been so cruelly and inexplicably abandoned, would regress right back to the way he'd been when I first met him. Only this time maybe worse. And perhaps by Christmas when I came back to him, he'd have become more unreachable himself. I knew that I must warn my friend and carefully prepare him for our separation, but each day I hesitated.

"I feel so well," I said to him instead, as if the saying of it made it so.

"I feel so amazingly well," I said repeatedly, and Henry nodded that he felt the same.

One morning Mrs. Cooley woke me early. She said she'd made an appointment for me to have a physical examination. Also, a dental check. I hadn't been looking well, she thought, and I'd been holding my jaw as if a tooth were bothering me. She'd asked me repeatedly about the tooth as well as my health. Because I wouldn't answer any of her questions, she'd felt it her duty to make the appointments for me.

"It won't take long, Paul," she insisted. "You'll feel much better when that tooth is fixed. It *has* been hurting you, hasn't it?" she said.

I looked away from her down at the floor. It was hard not speaking to Mrs. Cooley. I'd always liked her and thought she had a pleasant manner with the patients. When a man was well enough, she spoke to him as if he were an equal. It hurt me to be rude to her, but I didn't dare to risk it yet. There was no denying the improvement in my head since I had limited all conversation to the Baron.

As I left the ward with Mrs. Cooley, I was tempted to tell Henry where I was going. But it was early, and when I passed his room he was sleeping so soundly that I couldn't bring myself to wake him. I would have liked to leave a message for him with one of the orderlies, but I didn't see how this could be accomplished without talk.

There was a line of patients waiting to see Dr. Barber. I had to wait more than an hour for the physical examination. Outside the window I noticed that the morning had gone dark. The lawn was a sharp, electric green, and black storm clouds were moving swiftly in over the sky with a look of spreading gloom. Mrs. Cooley brought me a cup of coffee and a muffin, but I didn't touch them. I thought of Henry lying in his bed waiting for me with a puzzled, lost expression in his eyes. I paced the floor and watched the clock with an increasing sense of worry and impatience.

It was ten o'clock before I was able to see the dentist. While I sat in his chair thunder and lightning began. A high wind splattered rain against the windows. I thought I'd never see the rain come down so hard. The dentist extracted one of my teeth, but I felt no pain. I was thinking of Henry the whole time, knowing how worried he must be. I was half-sick thinking about it.

By the time I got to the ward it was close to noon. The Baron's bed was empty and his wheelchair was gone. I expected to find him in the dayroom, but he wasn't there. I checked all of the sleeping rooms along the hall, then went down to the cafeteria, stopped to look in the visitor's room and the recreation room. Two orderlies were playing ping pong, but no one else was there. I stepped outside. The rain had stopped and my heart jumped to see two deep wheel marks in the muddy ground by the front steps. It looked as if the Baron had shot his chair out the front door, cleared the steps, and landed violently on the rutted ground. I followed the wheel marks across the yard until they stopped in the driveway. The sky was beginning to clear and there was the sound of dripping by the buildings and the trees, and water gushing down the gutters by the road. The air was wonderfully fresh, as if it had been washed completely clean, and a strong wind blew with a surprising force. As I started down the hard-top path we'd often taken, I was trying to imagine in what spirit Henry had set out on his own. Whether he was perturbed or calm, and whether he'd gone looking for me, which seemed likely. I walked at a fast pace, but the Baron had gotten a good start on me. It was a half hour before I saw him on a path about a quarter mile ahead of me, moving along in an unhurried way. I felt delighted as a child to see him. I called his name, but the wind was blowing in my face. It swallowed up my voice. The Baron couldn't hear me, but I could see where he was going. He was almost at the point where the path drops sharply into a long sloping hill. At the bottom of this hill was the turnoff for the dirt path up to our cliff view. I walked faster and began to shout at him, but the Baron never slowed or turned in my direction. In fact to my dismay he picked up speed. There was a sudden urgency to the way he spun his wheels, and I saw the chair leap forward. As he started down the hill, he was racing. I was sure that he'd injure himself, and I began to run, still shouting to him. His head was bent so low that I could hardly see it, and he flew down the hill at a velocity that looked suicidal. I ran with all of my strength behind him and was relieved to see him make it to the bottom. "Henry, WAIT!" I called to him, but he pressed ahead as hard as ever. He crossed the grass at a good clip and started up the high dirt path churning his wheels. The wind veered around and blew behind me then. It seemed to push my back with great harsh shoves. I doubled my speed and by the time the Baron had begun to falter halfway up the hill, I caught up with him, grabbed his chair, and pushed it with one long-extended lunge up to the top and across the open patch of grass. My legs felt watery and strangely weak, and I collapsed on the wooden bench with a feeling of exhaustion so acute, I thought I might be sick. The Baron was just as winded. We sat heaving and gasping, unable to speak. Our mountain view was buried in dense fog. It was impossible to see the valley. My lungs hurt me and I felt pain in my shoulders, gripping my neck and rising to my head where the blood was beating in my ears. The wind was even stronger on the cliff. It came at us in little blasts. The Baron's face was still bent forward. There was something dejected about the way his back remained curved over and his hands stayed holding the arms of his chair.

"Why did you run away from me?" I asked at last. Henry didn't look at me or move.

"I'm sorry about this morning," I said. "They sent me to the doctor and the dentist very early. You were asleep. I didn't want to wake you." Henry raised his head. His eyes wee red. The misery in them was so intense, it shocked me. He didn't look at me. He stared out over the foggy trough of nothingness below and I could see that under his sadness was a layer of coldness and unforgiving distance he had made between us.

"There are some things I have to tell you. I should have told you long ago," I said. But the Baron remained stony and his aloofness made my words sound strangely foolish. I could almost sense that he was growing more distant from me by the minute, as if he were moving physically away from me again, and I'd begun to chase him. A gust of wind blew in my face. It whipped my hair and tugged at the strip of loosened bandage by the Baron's ear. I thought I heard somebody whisper, "Watch it, Paul. Just watch it." But the voice was pitiful and faint. The wind was stronger, lashing in my ears. It was blowing in my brain and all my thoughts were stirring, flying up and swirling in great arcs until my mind was spinning with them. I put my hands up to my face to stop the dizziness, the pressure and the knocking like great fists within my head. I reached for the Baron's arm. I held onto it and I let my head fall down until it touched his sleeve. I began to speak to him. I was crying, and the voice I used was alien to me. It was a terrible voice, hoarse and low, which seemed to rise from some deep suffocating chasm and had to wrench and choke itself in order to escape. Yet once the voice was started, on and on it went, like a machine switched on and driven separately from me. The words poured out with such a force, I felt I couldn't stop them if I tried. Words jumped out. Like things alive they leaped over each other in an effort for release. As they came, I heard the sound of drums begin, the noise of hurried marching feet, and a loud trumpet blast that sounded desperate, like a scream. Still my strange voice went on with the momentum of a river, and I told myself that if the army tried to overcome me, I would hurl myself over the cliff and wipe out the entire company in one grand explosion. Perhaps the General sensed the utter seriousness of my intention. The trumpet died away with a pathetic sigh, the drums and marching feet grew more remote and faint until I heard only the sound of my own stricken voice, this time more clearly. The grief was terrible in that weeping voice, so terrible there was nothing I could do but listen with a sense of growing recognition. I listened and I saw a little whitewashed farmhouse with two broken windows like two eyes, the door a gaping mouth wide open to the night. The house, set back from a dirt road, was vivid under the moon which also bathed the wide surrounding fields and all the trees along the road in ghostly light. There was a soldier hurrying up the road with a carbine rifle tightly clutched against his chest. He was whimpering to himself and moaning, his darting eyes alarmed and wide with fear. The smells of the Italian countryside were an assault of sweetness to his nose, and the beauty of the night was something incomprehensible and appalling to the soldier, mad and AWOL, running from his men who even now were searching for him down the road. He stopped before the small abandoned house, the dismal face whose window eyes looked balefully at him while he stared back with every nerve alert, the moonlight pouring down, the rifle tightly pressed in two white hands that shook and trembled with a constant agitation. There was an unexpected noise within the house, a shuffling in the dark. The startled soldier sprang into a crouch, his rifle swung out from his chest, and when he saw a flash of white go by the door, he shot. He kept on shooting even when he heard a woman's scream and didn't stop until his gun was empty. The company commander, Captain Barker, was running up the road. And there were others, one who took away his gun and one who ran up with a light and shone it on the dark-haired woman on the floor, thin and young, her white dress spattered with her blood, a child, a boy no more than nine, still clinging to her side, his body twitching, dying there before them. Captain Barker with a white ferocious face was saying, Christ, man, CHRIST look what you've done!"

From a far distance I could feel the Baron's hand. It rested like protection on my head while my own ragged voice went on. It was the voice of an exhausted child, monotonous and flat, a voice that was familiar to me now.

V

Did I dream it that the rain began to pour while Henry and I were still up on the cliff? I could remember so well the feeling of icy rain soaking my back and how it fell like walls around us. I quickly pushed the Baron down the hill. The ground was slippery and muddy. The rain was blinding and I almost fell. Henry pointed to the chapel and we hurried into it for shelter. Once inside, the Baron wheeled himself right up the aisle. He pointed with excitement to the little organ by the altar, one that I had never noticed before. He wanted to examine it more closely. I pushed him up the step and had to lift him to the organ bench. I was surprised to see how excited he was and pleased to see his old exuberance. When he pressed a G and heard the sound of it, he clapped his hands. He gestured to the little pew behind the organ and I sat there. Then, to my amazement, he began to play. Not haltingly or poorly as you would expect from a man with a damaged brain who'd never indicated that he knew an instrument. He played that organ easily and brilliantly, while I sat there levitated and transfixed. It seemed to me that I had never heard Bach played so well or Messiaen or Dupré. He played piece after piece. I told myself perhaps the beauty of the music was so overwhelming because I hadn't heard real music since the war, only the canned sound they play over the speakers on the wards. I told myself that I had lost the critical ability to judge the quality of his playing. But the Baron had started a Bach toccata, one that I knew well, and I felt the power of that piece played to its fullest glory, so it was the genius of the music that came through the self-effacing ease and excellence of Henry's playing. The rain had stopped and a ray of sun fell from the sacristy on Henry, shone on his graying head, flashed on his hands, and caught the dust that sparkled rising from the keys. He was playing flawlessly, and it was at that moment with a sense of creeping horror that I felt the hairs stand up on my neck. My eyes fell on the pumping feet and the helpless legs which leapt and danced over the pedals, and I had a sudden dead white feeling of pure fear that Henry Baron wasn't real.

❧❧ ❧❧ ❧❧

I woke up in a strange room. The sun was shining in my eyes. There was an old man asleep in the bed next to me. He had two tubes in his nose and his arm was hooked up to an IV. I was looking at him when my mother appeared beside the bed. Bill was standing beside her. She kissed my cheek and I smiled at her. "Don't try to speak, dear," she said, putting her hand over my mouth. "You've been very sick. The doctor wants you to rest and sleep as much as possible. Bill and I will be right here. Kathleen is coming, too. You must try to sleep now."

I closed my eyes. I dreamed I was back on the ward in Henry's room. Two nurses were about to change his bandages. I was anxious to leave the room, but the Baron indicated urgently that he wanted me to stay. I stood at the end of his bed while the nurses removed the bandages strip by strip, starting at the forehead. Henry kept his eyes on me, and I was anxious not to show the slightest shock at anything revealed. His cheek bones were uncovered and I saw his nose. It was exactly the nose I would have expected the Baron to have. And yet when I saw the lower half of my friend's face, I gasped. Where was the sunken hollow of the cheek, the sheared-off chin and the misshapen profile I'd so often seen? When the final swatch of bandage was removed, the face revealed was totally unmarred. I was reminded of Abe Lincoln when I saw the solemn dignity and the ugly beauty of the Baron's face. I stared at him and shook my head uncomprehendingly. "But why the bandages?" I asked. The Baron only smiled. This amazing man. He smiled.

When I woke up I was smiling, too. The room was dark and the old man was snoring loudly in the bed beside me. I kept thinking of Henry. I was remembering the way he'd played the organ in the chapel. Surely I must have dreamed it and the Baron must be real, I told myself, but I was afraid. Why was Henry's face still bandaged more than thirty years after the war? It seemed preposterous that I had never questioned it before. And why was it that in all the five months I had known him I could not remember any orderly or nurse ever referring to him or once saying the name of Henry Baron? Perhaps the army had made the Baron up just so that they could take him away from me. I suffered with my thoughts and never slept for the rest of the night. In the morning I was still awake when Mrs. Cooley walked into the room.

"I was one my way to work," she said cheerfully. "I'd have come to seen you sooner, but I was on vacation." She came over to the bed. I watched her, holding my breath, hoping she might mention Henry. She looked at me and her face became concerned. "Poor Paul. Have you been feeling awfully lonely?" She reached into her purse and dabbed my eyes and my face with Kleenex. I strained to speak, but Mrs. Cooley gripped my shoulder. "Don't Paul. You mustn't talk," she said. She looked alarmed. "Haven't they told you?" she said. "You've had a stroke. You'll be fine, but you can't speak yet. Your speech has been affected." I listened, stunned, while she went on to tell me about the therapy they'd be starting. I felt strangely like laughing, the bitter laugh that comes after despair, when the mind is worn out with pain and turns away from it with irony and cold amusement, when the chain of human moods begins to roll again, and life goes on and on.

The old man was gone from the bed beside me. I could hear my mother's voice out in the hall, talking to someone. The room was frightfully hot. A red-haired nurse came in and shut the window. "We're putting the air-conditioner on," she said. "You'll feel the difference soon." From where I lay the only view was one waving tree branch rising halfway up the window. The branch was heavy with dark leaves which were fully open and fully grown. I could see that it was a maple tree and that it was well into the summer. Time for my madness. Perhaps I was at this very moment mad, I thought. But then it came to me that there was no army, no sign of the army. The army was gone.

Ellen Wilbur

Ellen Wilbur is a prize winning fiction writer with work in the *Virginia Quarterly Review*, *Shenandoah*, *Ploughshares*, *The Georgia Review*, *Harvard Review*, *The Yale Review*, *Agni*, and *The Iowa Review* to name but a few.

She has won numerous literary awards including two **Pushcart Prizes**, and the **Emily Clark Balch Award for Fiction** given by *The Virginia Quarterly Review*.

Ellen was a **MacDowell Colony Fellow**, a **Radcliffe Bunting Institute Fellow**, recipient of an **Ingram Merrill Foundation Fellowship**, and the **St. Botolph Foundation Grant** for fiction.

She lives in Cambridge, Massachusetts.

Acknowledgments

I wish to thank the editors of the following publications, ordered by the year in which these stories first appeared:

"Wind and Birds and Human Voices" was published by *The Georgia Review* (1984). The story was reprinted in an anthology, *The Situation of the Story: Short Fiction in Contemporary Perspective*, (edited by Diana Young, St. Martin's Press, 1993.)

"Sundays" from the book won a Pushcart Prize 1985-86 edition. This story also appeared in *Wives and Husbands: 20 Stories About Marriage* (editors Michael Nagler and William Swanson) published by *New American Library*.

"The Critic" in *Harvard Review* (2000).

"Bed Check" in *The Yale Review* (2000).

"Rescue" in *The Georgia Review* (2001).

"Storms and Wars" in *The Iowa Review* (2006).

"Listening and Speaking" in *The Georgia Review* (2010).

"Fifteen" in *The Yale Review* (2010), a *Narrative Magazine* Story of the Week.

"Depression" in *Harvard Review* (2011)

"The Sailor" in *The Yale Review* (2014)

"The New Year" in *The Yale Review* (2016).

"The Fortune Teller" in *The Yale Review* (2018)

"Winter Scene" in *The Woven Tale Press* (fall, 2020)

Also by Ellen Wilbur

Fiction

◆ ◆ ◆

WIND AND BIRDS AND HUMAN VOICES
1st Edition, Hardback,
Stuart Wright Publishers, 1984
Paperback edition,
Plume-New American Library, 1985

Non-Fiction

◆ ◆ ◆

**THE CONSOLATIONS OF GOD:
GREAT SERMONS OF PHILLIPS BROOKS**
Ellen Wilbur, Editor
Eerdmans Pub Co, 2003

www.ingramcontent.com/pod-product-compliance
Lightning Source LLC
Chambersburg PA
CBHW021726190726

48289CB00008B/2718